My Little Secret

Also By Anna J.

Novels:

> *Get Money Chicks*
> *The Aftermath*
> *My Woman His Wife*

Short Story Compilations:

> *The Cat House*
> *Flexin' & Sexin': Sexy Street Tales Vol. I*
> *Fantasy*
> *Morning, Noon and Night:* "Can't Get Enough"
> *Fetish*
> *Stories to Excite You:* "Ménage Quad"

My Little Secret

a novel by

Anna J.

Q-Boro Books

An Urban Entertainment Company

Published by Q-Boro Books

Copyright © 2008 by Anna J.

ISBN : 978-1-60751-340-7

Printed in the United States of America

This is a work of fiction. It is not meant to depict, portray or represent any particular real persons. All the characters, incidents and dialogues are the products of the author's imagination and are not to be construed as real. Any references or similarities to actual events, entities, real people, living or dead, or to real locales are intended to give the novel a sense of reality. Any similarity in other names, characters, entities, places and incidents is en-tirely coincidental.

Q-BORO BOOKS
Jamaica, Queens NY 11434

Acknowledgments

I'm sitting here at two in the morning on a Friday night, and I'm supposed to be working on my already late manuscript, but my head is spinning. The year has just started, and I'm in the state of mind for change. The thing is, it kind of snuck up on me because I knew that I had some changes that needed to be made, but once I got to thinking I came to the realization that I had a lot going on. Not just your typical stuff either, but more so the way that I conduct business and myself, and some things were brought to my attention that knocked me off my square for a second. After talking to my favorite cousin on the phone for over an hour and both of us trying to come to some sort of plan, I realized that when more than one person tells you something about yourself some of it has to be true.

So although my day started with me waking up late for work, my car getting rear ended on the way to work, then finally getting to work and having to deal with people and say things to people that ultimately weren't an important factor in my life, it wasn't until now, at two in the morning when I should be sleeping, that I realized I had so much to be thankful for. I mean, I should be sleeping, but I want some ice cream and can't have it because I'm trying to get my figure back and I need to fit my clothes this summer. What's a girl to do?

Without God where would I be? Every time I think my life is just a wreck, I'm instantly thankful for the opportunity to be in a place in my life where, although I'm not sitting on top of the world, I'm certainly not buried six feet into it. At the times when I think my situation is beyond repair, I look back at so many other times when I didn't think I would get through something and I did. That's the way God works; it's just crazy that it took me thirty years to get that in my head.

Let me take this time now to thank all of my family for being supportive. Even the ones who hate on me and dog me behind my back. I never would have thought in a million years that I would be given an opportunity like this, and the few that support me without a doubt, I love you to death. It's hard being Super Woman when at times I need to break down and cry but can't. It's hard trying to stand in the face of my enemy and smile, especially when my enemy is my own flesh and blood, knowing about the phone calls and how I'm always the topic of conversation. The thing is, I forgive you. If Jesus Christ can forgive those who beat Him and hung Him from the cross, I know in my heart I can get past this. I won't mention any names, but do know that my love for my family is unwavering, even when it's not reciprocated.

Tisha, girl, we getting old. Remember back in the day when we got caught skipping school at Kingsessing playground and couldn't go skating for Halloween? We got in trouble like three years in a row, and the year we were finally able to go I broke my ankle. We've been through so much together. I've watched you grow to be an incredible mom and a wonderful person. I know you got a lot on your mind, and just understand that some people are only meant to be in your life for a season. A person can say whatever they want to say to you, but their actions say it all.

We're growing up, and it's scary as hell, but think about where we came from and where we are now. The sky's the limit. All you have to do is reach for it.

Janise, I remember when we met back in 1992 and we were new to Parkway. You were all shy and everything and I was all loud for no reason, but we formed a friendship that has stood the test of time. How many people have we both been cool with and here we are in 2008 and the rest of them are gone? You have a baby now, and I'm so happy for you. Thanks for being there all these years, and although we don't talk every day it's nice to know that at any given moment I can pick up the phone and you'll answer. I love you, girl!

Chereme, thank you for so many things. For being just a phone call away and allowing me to break down without judging me. For being one of the few people that call and ask me, am I okay and if I need something, even though you know if I needed it I would never say so. For being my friend, my sister, one of my biggest supporters, and never changing. We've known each other for about five years now, and if I had known how great of a friend you were back then I would have been made you my sister for life. I'm glad you're here now, though, and that's all that matters.

Shonda Whitten, let me take this time to apologize to you. When I came to your office that day and was all bent up and in tears because life was just getting to be too much you could have easily dismissed me and just kept it professional since you are the manager and have better things to do. Instead, you allowed me to close your office door and vent and cry and get out all of my frustrations, and at the same time gave me the soundest advice that

I've heard in a long time. After all of that when you recapped what I said to you the very first time we met I was shocked. Not at you, but at myself. First impressions are lasting, and even though I came at you sideways, you still made room in your heart to get to know me as a person. I apologize for our initial meeting, and I thank you for being the person you are and seeing me for the person I am. I'm in the midst of a transition, and I thank you for your patience.

Mark, Sabine, and Candace, we've come a long way since those *My Woman His Wife* days. Thanks for everything and for believing in me when I didn't believe in myself. Thanks for answering your phone while you're on vacation and office hours are over. The industry has changed so much over the years, and I'm glad to still be able to call Q-Boro Books family.

Tee C. Royal, you rocked these edits! I was so nervous about this project, but after receiving your honest feedback and suggestions I was instantly at ease. Congrats on your new addition, and thanks for just being an email/phone call away.

To the readers, thank you for all of the support, emails, interviews, and for spreading the word. Thanks to all the book clubs for the phone interviews, and letting me slide through to chill and chat with y'all. Cousin Vonnie, my new play cousin from MD, I haven't forgotten about you. You know how we do.

To all of the authors who are new to the game and those trying to get put on—Even those who have been here for a while, for some it was a matter of being in the right position at the right time. Just because you haven't been signed to a book deal doesn't mean you should give up. God doesn't make mistakes; so keep that in mind while you pursue your dreams.

It's now three-thirty in the morning, and through the tears and the smiles and the frowns I got through this like I'll be getting through 2008. Thanks to everyone for everything, and I'll see you at the top!

Anna J.

For every action, there is an equal and opposite reaction.
—*Newton's Third Law*

February 9, 2007

Ask Yourself

Jaydah

She feels like melted chocolate on my fingertips. The same color from the top of her head to the very tips of her feet. Her nipples are two shades darker than the rest of her, and they make her skin the perfect backdrop against her round breasts. Firm and sweet like two ripe peaches dipped in Baker's chocolate. They are a little more than a handful and greatly appreciated. Touching her makes me feel like I've finally found peace on earth, and there is no feeling in the world greater than that.

Right now her eyes are closed and her bottom lip is tightly tucked between her teeth. From my viewpoint between her widely spread legs I can see the beginnings of yet another orgasm playing across her angelic face. These are the moments that make it all worthwhile. Her perfectly arched eyebrows go into a deep frown, and her eyelids flutter slightly. When her head falls back I know she's about to explode.

I move up on my knees so that we are pelvis to pelvis.

Both of us are dripping wet from the humidity and the situation. Her legs are up on my shoulders, and her hands are cupping my breasts. I can't tell where her skin begins or where mine ends. As I look down at her and watch her face go through way too many emotions, I smile a little bit. She always did love the dick, and since we've been together she's never had to go without it.

I'm pushing her tool into her soft folds inch by inch as if it were really a part of me, and her body is alive. I say "her tool" because it belongs to her, and I enjoy using it on her. Her arms and legs wrap us in a cocoon of coconut oil and sweat, body heat and moisture, soft moans and teardrops, pleasure and pain, until we seemingly burst into an inferno of hot-like-fire ecstasy. Our chocolate skin is searing to the touch, and we melt into each other, becoming one. I can't tell where she begins . . . I can't tell where I end.

She smiles. Her eyes are still closed and she's still shaking from the intensity. I take this opportunity to taste her lips and to lick the salty sweetness from the side of her neck. My hands begin to explore, and my tongue encircles her dark nipples. She arches her back when my full lips close around her nipple, and I began to suck softly as if she's feeding me life from within her soul.

Her hands find their way to my head and become tangled in my soft wrap, identical to hers, but not as long. I push into her deep, and grind softly against her clit in search of her "J-spot" because it belongs to me, Jaydah. She speaks my name so softly, I barely hear her. I know she wants me to take what she so willingly gave me, and I want to hear her beg for it.

I start to pull back slowly, and I can feel her body tightening up, trying to keep me from moving. One of many soft moans is heard over the low hum of the clock radio that sits next to the bed. I hear slight snatches of Raheem DeVaughn singing about being in heaven, and I'm almost certain he wrote that song for me and my lady.

I open her lips so I can have a full view of her sensitive pearl. Her body quakes with anticipation from the feel of my warm breath touching it, my mouth just mere inches away. I blow cool air on her stiff clit, causing her to tense up briefly, her hands taking hold of my head, trying to pull me closer. At this point my mouth is so close to her, all I have to do is twitch my lips to make contact. But I don't. I want her to beg for it.

My index finger is making small circles against my own clit, my honey sticky between my legs. The ultimate pleasure is giving pleasure, and I've experienced that on both accounts. My baby can't wait anymore, and her soft pants are turning into low moans. I stick my tongue out, and her clit gladly kisses me back.

Her body responds by releasing a syrupy-sweet slickness that I lap up until it's all gone, fucking her with my tongue the way she likes it. I hold her legs up and out to intensify her orgasm because I know she can't handle it that way.

"Does your husband do you like this?" I ask between licks. Before she can answer, I wrap my full lips around her clit and suck her into my mouth, swirling my tongue around her hardened bud, causing her body to shake.

Snatching a second toy from the side of the bed, I take one hand to part her lips, and I ease her favorite toy (The Rabbit) inside her. Wishing that the strap-on I was wearing was a real dick so I could feel her pulsate, I turn the toy on low at first, wanting her to receive the ultimate pleasure. In the dark room the glow-in-the-dark toy is lit brightly, the light disappearing inside her when I push it all the way in.

The head of the curved toy turns in a slow circle while the pearl beads jump around on the inside, hitting up against her smooth walls during insertion. When I push the toy in, she pushes her pelvis up to receive it. My mouth is latched on to her clit like a vise. She moans louder, and I kick the toy up a notch to medium, much to her delight. Removing my mouth from her clit, I rotate between flicking my wet tongue across it to heat it and blowing my breath on it to cool it, bringing her to yet another screaming orgasm, followed by strings of "I love you" and "Please don't stop."

Torturing her body slowly, I continue to stimulate her clit, while pushing her toy in and out of her in a constant rhythm. When she lifts her legs to her chest I take the opportunity to let the ears on the rabbit toy that we are using do its job on her clit while my tongue finds its way to her chocolate ass. I bite one cheek at a time, replacing each bite with wet kisses, afterward sliding my tongue in between to taste her there. Her body squirming underneath me lets me know I've hit the jackpot, and I fuck her with my tongue there also.

She's moaning, telling me in a loud whisper that she can't take it anymore. That's my cue to turn the toy up high. The buzzing from the toy matches that of the radio, and with her moans and my pants mixed in, we sound like a well-rehearsed orchestra singing a symphony of passion. I allow her to buck against my face while I keep up with the rhythm of the toy, her juices oozing out the sides and forming a puddle under her ass. My lips taste salty-sweet from kissing her body. I'm loving it.

She moans and shakes until the feeling in the pit of her stomach subsides and she is able to breathe at a normal rate. I know exactly how she feels because I get that very same feeling upon orgasm when she's blessing me. She tries to get her head together, rubbing the sides of my body up and down in a lazy motion, and I take that opportunity to milk the rest of her orgasm from her body before I lay back to relax.

Valentine's Day is fast approaching, and I have a wonderful evening planned for the two of us. She already promised me that her husband wouldn't be an issue because he'll be out of town that weekend, and besides all that, they haven't celebrated Cupid's day since the year after they were married, so I didn't even think twice about it. After seven years it should be over for them anyway.

"It's your turn now," she says to me in a husky, lust-filled voice, and I can't wait for her to take control.

She starts by rubbing her oil-slicked hands over the front of my body, taking extra time around my sensitive nipples before bringing her hands down across my flat stomach. I've removed the strap-on dildo, and am completely naked under her hands.

I can still feel her sweat on my skin, and I can still taste her on my lips. Closing my eyes, I enjoy the sensual massage I'm being treated to. After two years of us making love it's still good and gets better every time.

She likes to take her time covering every inch of my body, and I enjoy letting her. She skips past my love box and starts at my feet, massaging my legs from the toes up.

When she gets to my pleasure point, her fingertips graze the smooth, hairless skin there, quickly teasing me before she heads back down and does the same thing with my other limb. My legs are spread apart and lying flat on the bed with her in between, relaxing my body with ease. A cool breeze from the cracked window blows across the room every so often, caressing my erect nipples, making them harder than before, until her hands warm them back up again.

She knows when I can't take anymore, and she rubs and caresses me until I am begging her to kiss my lips. I can see her smile through half-closed eyelids, and she does what I request. Dipping her head down between my legs, she kisses my lips just as I asked, using her tongue to part them so she can taste my clit. My body goes into mini-convulsions on contact, and I am fighting a battle to not cum—a battle I never win.

"Valentine's Day belongs to us, right?" I ask her again between moans. I need her to be here. V-Day is for lovers. She and her husband haven't been that in ages. I deserve it . . . I deserve her. I just don't want this to be a repeat of Christmas or New Year's Eve.

"Yes, it's yours," she says between kisses on my thigh and sticking her tongue inside of me. Two of her fingers find their way inside of my tight walls, and my pelvic area automatically bounces up and down on her hand as my orgasm approaches.

"Tell me you love me," I say to her as my breathing becomes raspy. A fire is spreading across my legs and working its way up to the pit of my stomach. I need her to tell me before I explode.

"I love you," she says, and she places her tongue in my slit, and I release my honey all over her tongue.

It feels like I am on the Tea Cup ride at the amusement park as my orgasm jerks my body uncontrollably and it feels like the room is spinning. She is sucking and slurping my clit while the weight of her body holds the bottom half of me captive. I'm practically screaming and begging her to stop, and just when I think I'm about to check out of here, she lets go of my clit.

I take a few more minutes to get my head together, allowing her to pull me into her and rub my back. We lay like that for a little while longer, listening to each other breathe, and much to my dismay she slides my head from where it is resting on her arm and gets up out of the bed.

I don't say a word. I just lie on the bed and watch her get dressed. I swear, everything she does is so graceful, like there's a rhythm riding behind it.

Pretty soon she is dressed and standing beside the bed, looking down at me. She smiles and I smile back, not worried because she promised me our lover's day, and that's not quite a week away.

"So, Valentine's Day belongs to me, right?" I ask her again, just to be certain.

"Yes, it belongs to you."

We kiss one last time, and I can still taste my honey on her lips. She already knows the routine, locking the bottom lock behind her.

Just thinking about her makes me horny, so I pick up her favorite toy to finish the job. Five more days, and it'll be on again.

February 14, 2007

Miss Stress

Jaydah

I can't believe this bitch had the nerve to stand me up, again. After all I've done for her, she just keeps running back to the arms of that loser. For what reason, I'm still trying to figure out. Okay, so he's a doctor and he provides her with a lavish lifestyle, but all of that means absolutely nothing if that bedroom ain't hitting for nothing. How does this guy don the title of Chief of Gynecology and he can't even make his own wife cum? That's why she keeps bringing her behind to see me.

I've heard her say on so many occasions how she is so fed up with his lack of length and stamina, but my whole thing is, she knew that shit before she married him. What the hell did she think? His dick was going to grow after they exchanged vows? And since we're being real about some things, good head will only get you so far. I don't have time to be getting all hot and bothered just to be let down by spontaneous combustion on his part. Damn, can I at least get my nut first?

I'm even more pissed that I'm sitting out here in the damn rain in front of their house. She doesn't know I know where she lives. Yet. So let's just keep that our little secret.

It's chilly as hell in this car, but I don't want to draw attention to myself in this haughty-ass neighborhood. It's bad enough I paid my cousin to let me borrow her old dusty Honda to come over here. I don't want to blow my cover by making any unnecessary noise from her loud-ass engine.

My stomach knots up every time I see them embrace, and watching them through these binoculars is starting to give me a damn headache. Does that bitch have on the lingerie I bought her for her birthday? Lord, let my eyes be deceiving me because I'd hate to have to bust up in there on their asses.

Then she keeps smiling and giggling and shit, like they're just having a dazzling muthafuckin' time. Just two weeks ago she was telling me that having sex with him was like watching paint dry. Paint? You've got to be fucking kidding me. I had more fun at my grandmother's funeral, so something has to give.

We were supposed to be spending Valentine's Day together. The plan was to meet her at Suburban Station, and we would take a horse and carriage ride around Love Park. From there we would be dropped off at *Panache*, where we would feed each other French delicacies over a candlelit dinner. Afterward, that expensive-ass horse and carriage ride would drop us off at the Hyatt down on Delaware Avenue, where I reserved the presidential suite for the next two days. It was then that I would introduce her to a whole new way of having those multiple orgasms that she loves so much.

She promised me for the billionth time that everything was a go and that nothing would hold us back. Not even her trifling-ass husband, Ray. It hasn't been quite a week since we've seen each other, but I knew some shit had gone down because she had been ignoring me since Monday.

When she was at my house Sunday night, barely breathing because I was putting the smackdown on that ass, it was all good. I had her from behind with nine inches inside her, and another of our toys in the back door. She was throwing it back, and I was catching that shit like I was a damn baseball player on third base.

"Your husband doesn't do this for you, does he?"

"No, baby, not like this," she said with her eyes closed.

She was probably biting her bottom lip out of habit, and I was surprised she had any lip left. I was rubbing my finger across her clit, and pinching her nipples at the same time with my free hand, while working the shit out of this strap-on. She was begging me to let her turn over on her back, but we'd do that on my time.

"Is that right? Turn that ass over and spread 'em."

She obliged without hesitation, and I was back in there like I'd never left. She had an angelic, peaceful look on her face like she was in heaven at that very moment.

The amazing thing about a dick is you can buy exactly the size you want just about anywhere. If only I could actually pee while standing, I'd be on point. But I know the power the penis has behind it, especially one that doesn't ever go down.

"Yes, just like that."

I was killing her with deep strokes. I had her legs spread as wide as humanly possible and her toes pointing at the ceiling, with both of her nipples in my mouth. Her skin felt just as soft as mine, if not softer, and I tasted a hint of coconut from the flavored body crayons we'd used earlier in the evening. If nothing else, I made sure she got what she wasn't getting at home. Her husband could never compete with me.

"Come on, ride mommie's dick."

I lay down on the bed, and she pounced on me like the lioness I made her into. She rocked back and forth on the entire nine inches the strap-on had to offer while I fingered her clit and continued to suck on her nipples. She had her head thrown back and her eyes closed, indicating that an eruption was about to occur.

"Come on, cum on mommie's dick," I whispered to her in a soft voice, meeting her stroke for stroke. I could feel my own orgasm getting closer, and I didn't think I would be able to hold it.

All of a sudden her entire body stiffened, and she wrapped her arms and legs around me real tight. I enjoyed the view and feel of her honey running down the sides of my tool and forming puddles on both sides of my legs. Lord, when this girl exploded it was serious business.

"So, Valentine's Day belongs to us, right?"

"Yes, it's just me and you."

My dumb ass fell for the okey-doke again. She did the same shit on my birthday, and at this point I am tired. I've been watching them act a fake-ass fool for the past three hours, and now it's time to make it right.

I make sure the car is out of sight before I get out and make my way up the winding walkway to the Hunter estate. Looking behind me to make sure no big-ass dogs run up on me, I finally get to the door and am able to ring the bell. Checking my makeup in the doorknocker, I know that everything is on point, and the look on Midori's face will be priceless. After I ring the bell twice, one of the lovebirds finally comes to the door.

"Hi, may I help you?" Ray says once the door was completely open.

I can see inside their home. I must say, their crib is laid.

"Hello, sir. I'm sorry to bother you. It's just that my car broke down right down the road, and my cell phone is dead. Is it possible I could use your phone to call triple A?"

He looks at me like he's skeptical at first, but I allow my trench coat to slip open some, allowing him a peek at my naked flesh. Yep, I am a damn fool for being outside in the middle of February in nothing but a trench coat, thong, and heels, but I'm not thinking about all of that.

"Honey, who's at the door?"

I hear my lover of the past two years call out from somewhere in the house, and it takes everything in me to keep my face straight.

"Ummm, it's—forgive me, but I didn't get your name."

"Oh, it's ummm . . . Sarah," I say, opting to use a fake name. I don't want her to know it's me until I am inside her house and in her face.

"It's Sarah, sweetheart. She's having car trouble and

needs to use the phone." Ray ushers me in, directing me to follow him to the back of the house toward the kitchen.

I'm in awe at the spread they have here, but I have to keep up appearances.

"Sarah from the Johnson household? Why would she be knocking on our door this time of"—She stops dead in her stride when she emerges from the kitchen and sees me standing here.

"Sarah, this is my lovely wife, Midori. She was just making some tea. Why don't you have a seat while I get you a cup and the phone. You might as well wait in here until they come. It is too chilly outside to sit in your car."

He doesn't even wait for an answer; he just walks away and I take a seat. I make sure to show Midori my thong before closing my coat properly. She looks like she is ready to piss on herself, and I have to use all of my strength to hold my laugh in.

"What are you doing here? How did you know where I lived?" Midori speaks to me in a low whisper through clenched teeth. She looks like she's ready to knock me dead out of my chair, but ask me if I give a damn.

"How was I supposed to know this was your house? I'm having car trouble and randomly knocked on a door."

"How in hell are you having car trouble and you just got a 2007 Maxima? What kind of shit are you trying to—"

"Sarah, here is the phone. I have triple A on the line. I have a good friend who works over there. Just explain the problem and he'll be here in no time." Ray offers me the phone and the cup of tea, and I take both.

After explaining the make-believe trouble I was having, I hang up the phone and watch Midori with an amused look on my face. Ray just stands there looking at the both of us, not sure what to do next. If he's like any other man, he's probably picturing us in a threesome, something that will never happen.

"Uh, Sarah, would you like for me to take your coat?"

"No, actually I'm okay. Your friend said he wouldn't take long." I offer him a fake smile. I should take the shit off and let her dumb ass see what she's missing, but I have to be mature about this.

We sit around and hold light conversation, and I ask them questions about their marriage that I already know the answers to, just to see if they will lie. Of course they do, and that just makes the situation that much more interesting. From what Midori used to say, you would think they were ten steps away from a divorce, but at this moment they act like they live the perfect gotdamned life.

Soon after, Ray's AAA friend comes, and I feign innocence when he puts the key in the ignition and the car starts right up.

"Thank you so much, again, for your help. How can I repay you?"

"Well, we are having a birthday party for my wife on the twenty-second, and I would be honored to have you as a guest. Here's my card."

"The twenty-second of this month?" I ask with a puzzled look on my face while taking the card. All this time she had me thinking her birthday was in May, and here it is he's about to celebrate it in a matter of days.

"Yes, my lovely wife here will be turning thirty-seven, and we have a gala event planned. So I hope to see you there."

"Oh, you will. I always keep my promises," I reply, making sure to make direct eye contact with Midori before turning away.

I stick the card in my pocket before making myself comfortable inside my cousin's compact car, and make my way slowly down the road. I can see Midori and Ray in my rearview mirror up until I go over the hill. I'm not sure if I can forgive Midori after this one. Let's just say, she'll have a lot of making up to do.

Mrs. Hunter

Midori

Iam ready to fucking scream! What kind of person just tracks you down and shows up at your house unexpectedly? She must think I was born yesterday if she expects me to believe that she "randomly" picked my house out of all of the damn houses on this street. I should have left her ass alone a year ago, but what is a girl to do? I have an orgasm fetish, and my husband isn't able to do anything about it.

Then, as if the situation isn't awkward enough, Ray's dumb ass invites her to my birthday party. Now I have to try and explain why I'm celebrating my May 15 birthday on February 22. I swear he doesn't think sometimes. All he probably saw was titties and ass anyway, and was looking for a new piece to show off to his boring doctor friends.

If he thinks it's going down like that, he is sadly mistaken. Jaydah belongs to me. I just have to make things right again.

I know she's pissed, but the entire situation was out of

my control. I thought for sure I saw a conference listed on Ray's planner. Maybe that was just to throw me off from this little surprise celebration. I couldn't call the hotel because everywhere I went in the house he was right on my heels. It made me start to wonder if he knew that I was cheating. Besides, we hadn't celebrated Valentine's Day since the year after we wedded, and we've been married for nine years! So, I'm sure you can imagine my surprise.

It wasn't like I didn't want to celebrate, but after years of going all out to make it a special day for us, only for Ray to have an impromptu meeting or to suddenly stay late at work made me let it all go.

That was until I met Jaydah two years ago. I usually spent my holidays with her when Ray wasn't dragging me to functions or wanting to keep up appearances at his parents' house. On a few occasions he surprised me with a change of plans, but I always made it up to Jaydah.

I was shocked to see her in my house, but I instantly felt bad when she revealed the thong set that I bought her. I knew her well enough to know that she never even stepped into the bra, and that thong was all she had on under that trench coat.

Of course I played my part. I had to. He couldn't know that she was the one occupying my time on those nights when he wanted to do his thing. Hell, I'm entitled to some satisfaction, right? I could see the hurt in her eyes when her car started and she had to go. I wanted to take her into my arms right then, but I couldn't. Being Ray Hunter's wife definitely has benefits, and I'm not letting a woman who can use the hell out of a dildo fuck that up for me. Being a pediatrician pays well too, and as they say, two incomes are always better than one.

We waited until we couldn't see her car anymore to go back in the house. I know Ray's mind was ticking, but I'd be damned if I'd initiate the conversation. I wonder if he heard us arguing while he was in the kitchen. Even if he did, a part of me hoped he won't bring it up because I'd have to lie about the shit, and I don't feel like all that right now.

I straighten up the kitchen and make sure all of the lights are out before I go upstairs. When I walk into the bedroom, Ray is stretched out on the bed with a glass of chardonnay in one hand and his dick in the other. I must admit, Ray isn't long and thick like the toys Jaydah and I use, but he isn't all that small either. I guess you could say he has an average-sized dick. Real average. Like five and a half inches or so, but it was thick with a fat mushroom head that made its presence known. That really wasn't a problem, though. If he could just last a little longer and learn how to use it we'd be "in like Flynn", and I wouldn't have to step outside the box.

As I approach the bed, I see he has a look in his eyes that I've never noticed before. Could it be that he is picturing Jaydah, or Sarah if she tells it? He is definitely standing at attention, so I decide to get this over with as soon as possible.

I make a big deal out of taking off the wife-beater and lace boy shorts I have on under my bathrobe. Rubbing on my nipples and rotating my hips to the smooth jazz that is playing on the radio, I lift the shirt over my head and palm both breasts à la Janet Jackson from the front of her *Janet* CD cover. His face remains the same, and I continue with my show.

I turn around and bend over so he can get a good view of my pussy, before removing my panties and tossing them to the side. I'm wet as hell, but it isn't for him. If we were thinking of the same person, that might make the sex a little better.

I move around to the side and step up on the bed, positioning myself over his erection. It isn't much to slide down on, but I come down on him slow and hard, taking him on with ease. I start to ride him, making sure to press my clit against his pelvis because, Lord knows, he isn't long enough to reach my G-spot.

He surprises me by taking his glass and pouring some of his drink over my nipples. He shocks me even more when he takes them into his mouth, and repeats the act until all of it is gone. I'm still riding him, and my natural juices mixed with remnants of his chardonnay make for an interesting sensation against my skin.

I push down harder, so I can feel him deeper. To my surprise, he hasn't cum yet, and we are already three minutes into our session.

He sets the glass on the nightstand and palms both of my breasts, kissing one nipple then the other, then both at the same time.

I lean back to get a good look at him, because I'm almost certain I was in bed with another man.

He takes one hand and spreads the lips of my pussy and uses his thumb to make small circles on my clit.

I'm not sure if it is this newfound freak in my husband or the surprise of the evening that makes me cum so hard, but I think for sure my heart is going to jump out of my chest and sprint halfway across town from the excitement.

"This feel good to you?" Ray asks me in a tone I've never heard before in all the years we've been married.

I can't get my tongue to form an answer, but my mind is certainly spiraling out of control.

"Does this feel good to you?" he asks in a forceful tone, grabbing my hips and pounding into me like he is going to pop out of my forehead.

Damn, I was not expecting this, but I hope it stays. "Yes, it feels good," I moan out, holding on to his chest for support because he turned into a stallion out of nowhere.

"Turn that ass over and give me my pussy."

I hop my ass off him and turn the other way on all fours, my feet hanging off the edge of the bed. He stands behind me and rubs the head of his dick against my clit, and I want to scream because it feels so good. I think he's going to slide in, and my walls are contracting, ready to receive him.

Instead, he drops down behind me and puts his tongue in me, using his middle finger to stimulate my clit. I'm falling out on some real white girl porn shit, because I can't believe my husband has me twisted like this. I beg him for mercy and explode all in his mouth.

He finally obliges and gives me the dick. He has my ass cheeks spread, and is in me so deep, I think for sure my wish came true and he grew a couple of inches. He puts his finger in my ass, and pumps it to the same rhythm as his dick.

How does he know I like double entry? We've never gone that route before, but better late than never. I'm not mad at all.

Next thing I know, time stands still for all of five seconds and he is tapping on my G-spot like a man with a power drill. My entire body spazzes out of control, and I'm running like a faucet turned on full blast all down his length, and the inside of my thighs.

"That's right, cum on daddy's dick."

I don't know where this new husband of mine came from. I'm not sure if it is the alcohol or Jaydah's impromptu visit, but I'll have his ass drinking and around half-naked women all the time if that's what it takes to get a good lay out of him.

He allows me to turn over on my back, and he gets on his knees, bringing my body at waist level with his. He pulls a vibrator from under the pillow, and in no time flat he is stroking me with his dick in the anal entry and using the dildo inside my pussy. My legs are behind my head, and my knees are pressed against the sides of my face, as I enjoy this sexual beatdown. He is tearing some shit up, and I'm enjoying every minute of it.

"Tell me it's mine," he says in a husky tone, working me over like a professional.

I try to wrap my mind around the change of events, but I can't get it together. "It's yours!"

"What's mine?" he asks, pushing deeper on both ends.

That tingling sensation that I only get with Jaydah is starting at my toes and working its way up. "This pussy. It's yours."

"It's mine, huh? What else is mine?" he asks, speeding up the pace a little, and now rubbing on my clit with his free hand.

That's too much going on at one time, and I damn near lose it. "All of me . . . whenever you want it," I reply, out of breath. It's hard for me to control my orgasm and talk. One has to give, because I am about to lose it.

"Is that so?" he says, moving faster inside me and across my clit.

"Yes! It's all yours."

"Can I cum now?" he asks, pumping into me at top speed.

I'm about to explode my damn self, so we might as well do it together. "Yes, cum with me."

He pumps into both holes at an erratic pace, satisfying both of us in a matter of seconds. My legs are still shaking from the impact as he lays his head on my chest to catch his breath.

We stay like that for about five minutes before we get up to shower. The action continues in there, and I am almost convinced that our marriage can actually work.

After taking turns lotioning each other down, we get into the bed in the spoon position, and he strokes my stomach until we fall asleep. The last thing I remember hearing him say is that we should start to think about having children. I don't know if I am hearing him correctly because I am half 'sleep, but I decide to revisit that situation in the morning.

To my surprise I get up at eight o' clock. While Ray showers and dresses, I am in the kitchen cooking like I was Whoopi Goldberg in *The Color Purple* and Shug Avery had just gotten in town. I have hotcakes, sausage, eggs, biscuits, and freshly squeezed orange juice all served with a fresh cup of hazelnut coffee and his morning paper ready for him when he comes downstairs. He smiles while he eats, and I am tempted to move that plate out of the way and be his breakfast, but I hold it down.

I don't bring up the kids thing from last night, but we

will definitely talk about it soon. After kissing him good-bye, I go upstairs to wash and dress myself. I have to get to the office by ten, and it's already nine o'clock. I'll deal with Jaydah, too. First I have to make sure that this new husband stays before I let her go.

If You Think You're Lonely Now . . .

Jaydah

Wait until you're truly by yourself in a dark-ass condo mad as hell because the one person who is supposed to love you unconditionally already belongs to someone else. And I swear I tried so many times to just walk away from it all, but the more I think about it, the more I wonder if I should. I mean, I'm the one who holds her and makes her feel wanted while her husband practically lives at the office. She didn't know satisfaction until she met me, and now I get the short end of the stick? I must be a damn fool or whipped, or both, but I'm not taking this lying down.

Little does the good Dr. Hunter know, I've just declared war. There's no real competition, because I've got dude by a long shot, and I don't even have a real dick. If I play my cards right, Midori will belong to me and no one else. After all, my dick is bigger anyway. For right now, I'm going to chill in this tub and wait for her to call, because I know she will.

So, her birthday is in a week, huh? That lying bitch. I should've whipped her ass on the spot just because, but I'll keep my cool. I'll just take it out on her ass when she gets here. I'm still trying to figure out why she felt like she had to lie, as if deceiving her husband wasn't enough. Here I am being straight-up about everything, and I couldn't even get a real birthdate out of the bitch. Just when you think you know someone, you realize you don't know them at all.

It has already been three days since the entire incident at her house, but I'm sure she's playing hard to get. For a second, it really looked like they were happy together. Maybe I'm kidding myself by thinking she and I have something. Who's to say that I am anything more than a smash? At the same time, she's told me that she loved me on so many occasions. Or does she really just love the dick-down that I've been giving her? If that's the case, it'd truly be fucked-up, and she will pay.

I'm not a toy to be played with, and then when you're done, you put me back on the shelf. She can't honestly tell me that she felt nothing after all this time. All the tears I've wiped away and all of the orgasms had to count for something, right? Then again, she lied about something as petty as her birthday, so how can I tell?

I saw how her husband was looking at me, too. I thought for a second I saw his tongue fall out of his mouth. Just like a damn dog. Maybe he could be of use. If I can get him too—man, what am I doing? I just need to get shit right with Midori, but the idea of stringing them both along does sound appealing.

I've been staring at his business card for a while now. Since he was so gracious to invite me to her birthday party,

I will certainly be there, and I'll be the flyest thing walking. I have this hot little black dress that will have the heads of both men and women turning.

Okay, so it's ten o'clock now. I know I need to stop by my publicist's house before I go to that book signing tomorrow. I guess it would be wise to get my clothes together now, but what do I wear? I'm really ready to go to Midori's house and act a fool, but I'll stay cool. Shit will be hitting the fan sooner than anticipated, and she'll have no choice but to decide.

It's funny because when I met her two years ago at the signing I had at the Borders bookstore in the Gallery she said she enjoyed my book, but couldn't see herself going out like the wife did in my fictional tale. I remember it like it was yesterday.

"Jaydah, it is so nice to meet you. I have to tell you that I really enjoyed your book."

"That's always good to hear. Do you want me to sign your copy?" By this time I was just checking her out, and she was definitely on point. People ask me all the time if my book is based on a true story, and I'm not lying by telling them no, but in her case I'd make an exception.

"Sure, and make sure to include your number. I've been looking for someone to tell my story for the longest, and I think you would do a perfect job."

"How you figure?" I asked, now intrigued by what she had to say. Most people are against the whole girl-on-girl thing, but this one seemed to appreciate it.

"Okay, for starters, the wife had no business allowing her husband to invite some chick into their relationship. That was just dumb on her part. Secondly, if you are going to creep out on your husband with a woman, at least have the decency to come home with your panties on."

I laughed a little and continued to autograph her book. I wondered briefly if she was married, but then decided it didn't matter. She was on point, and I'd be making it a point to get in them panties soon.

"So, what exactly did you find odd about it? That happens every day in someone's life," I replied as a stall tactic to keep her at my table. Her eyes held me captive, and my thong was getting soaked by the second.

"It wouldn't have gone down in my household like that. My husband better not even fix his mind to bring some chick home."

"But would you?" I asked her, a dare behind the statement. I would know exactly what was up with her by the way she answered my question.

"Not sure that I would. If I were to step out with a woman, I wouldn't bring her home. I'd take her some place where we could do our thing and my husband wouldn't find out."

"So, you would do it?" I asked again, just to make sure I heard her right. Let me find out this chick was an undercover closet lesbo. People be thinking that these books are fiction, but most of the stories out here are true to the game.

"Ummm . . . when does the sequel to this come out? I need to find out what happens with that married couple. The way she caught her husband was truly compromising."

"It will be out sometime during the fall of next year, but I can help you with your book before that. Here is my card. Make sure you use it."

"I will . . . definitely," she said, looking at the card then tucking it in her purse.

At that point I was ready to leave the signing and scoop her up, but I was cool. She would call soon, and it would-n't be about a damn book.

Wow, that was two years ago, and it all came to this. Where is the respect? She acts like we've never been through anything. She was there for my book release party and everything, and all this time she's been lying to me. I'm not sure I can let that shit go, and I have to get her back. I will tear that ass up one last time, though.

I wonder if her husband knows that the tattoo she has on her shoulder is really my name written in Chinese. Does he know that I put passion marks on the inside of her thighs so he won't see them, and that the reason why they couldn't have sex for their ninth anniversary wasn't because her period was on? I fucked her so long and hard, she was sore, and it hurt just for her to open her legs up.

The more I think about, it the madder I'm getting, and right now I don't need that kind of stress. I have a radio interview first thing Friday morning that I'm nervous as hell about, and I start my next book tour in a matter of weeks.

On my last tour I was stroking her ass in every state, and now I'm feeling that it won't be going down like that this time. Then I have a deadline to meet with my next book that my publisher done called me about at least six times in the last week. I swear I don't need this kind of stress right now. All I want to do is lie in Midori's arms and feel that everything is okay in the world. It's hard being Jaydah B., and she of all people should know that.

I'm Never Keeping Secrets, and I'm Never Telling Lies . . .

Midori

"**I** wanna make it up to you," I say softly into the phone. I'm in my office taking a brief break between patients. It has been a tiring day, and I'm really not in the mood for any drama. I wanted to at least see how Jaydah was acting so I would know if it was a good idea to go over there after work or not.

It's been about four days since she popped up at my house, and truth be told, I am still a little upset about that shit. I have never taken her anywhere within a ten-mile radius of my home, so that meant she was getting information on me from other sources. To say I'm not cool with that is putting it mildly. At the risk of making myself look suspect in front of my husband, I was ready to knock the shit out of her, but I refrained. Lucky her.

"Make it up, Midori?—If that's your real name," Jaydah says, spitting venom into the phone like she hates my very existing. "You lied about something as petty as the day you were born. I can't trust a word that comes out of your mouth now."

"I know I fucked up, okay. I know, but you at least owe it to me to explain myself."

"I don't owe you shit, but we'll see how it goes down on your birthday."

"So, you're actually going to come to the party?" I ask in a desperate voice.

"You better believe it. And not the fake-ass birthday you told me about that was supposed to be in May. Look, I got a book that I need to work on. I'll see you there."

She hangs up before I can say anything else, and I guess I deserve it. Coming to the party is one of the things I want to talk to her about. I don't need her in the same room as my husband. I've told her too many secrets, and we've shared too much for her to be in his presence. I don't need shit to slip out. My livelihood could be at stake here.

I start to call her back, but I know it would be useless. When Jaydah gets into a zone, all I can do is wait until she calms down. If I didn't have an office to run, I would leave at this very moment and go over to talk to her.

I hate that I am stressing her out because I know how she gets when she's trying to write, and she doesn't need me feeding her any bullshit. Our arguing was the entire reason behind her missing her deadline twice to turn in the last book, and I don't want to be the cause of her messing up this time around.

Valentine's Day was so important to Jaydah, and I was actually excited about spending it with her. The year before she gave me an engagement ring, but I wore it on the other hand because the rings my husband gave me occupied the finger on my left. I was honestly surprised that my husband stuck around for the holiday, but I will say I ended up pleasantly surprised.

I have seven days before my party to talk her into staying home. Fuck it—I'll be going straight there when I leave here. By then I'll know what I need to say to her to get things back on track. Maybe I'll buy her something from Victoria's Secret. She loves lingerie.

Scooping up charts from my desk for the patients I had for the rest of the afternoon, I take one last sip of my now cold coffee, determined to get through these last few appointments before I head out.

Before I can leave the office the phone rings. I start to not answer it because nine times out of ten it was probably a parent wanting to talk about their child, but then again it could be Jaydah calling back, and I need to talk to her. On the third ring I scoop up the receiver, pressing it to my ear and hoping the caller hasn't already hung up the phone.

"Woodland Pediatrics. Midori Hunter speaking, how may I help you?" I ask, hoping it was Jaydah telling me I could stop by.

"Hey, sexy," my husband speaks into the phone, turning my stomach instantly.

In all of the years we've been married, I can count on one hand, not including my thumb, how many times he's called me at work. I just assumed he was too busy fucking the medical assistants who worked at his office to worry about calling me. I saw how some of them used to look at me when I came in there, but I didn't care. He didn't give a damn about any of them, since we're being real about some shit. All they were was a quick fuck on one of the exam tables after hours. I, on the other hand, wear his ring and live in his house. I will never be replaced, no matter how much they want me to be gone.

"Hey, Ray. What did I do to deserve this call?" I ask, faking like I was happy to hear from him. I hope he isn't calling to talk about that little slip-up the other night. We are not ready for kids, and I am hoping he was just talking in the heat of the moment.

"Since when did I need a reason to call my wife?" he asks somewhat seriously, but I can tell he is trying to make light of the situation. "I was calling to see what time you were leaving the office. A few of my colleagues and I are meeting over at Bone Fish for drinks and dinner, and I wanted you to join us."

"Today?" I ask, stalling him for a few seconds. I'm tied because Ray is making an effort to get our life back on track, but thoughts of Jaydah keep tugging at the back of my mind. Although the relationship I maintain with my husband is more important, I need Jaydah for different reasons, and I'm not ready to let her go just yet.

"Umm, yeah, that would be today. Why? Are you stuck at the office?"

"No, I'm not stuck. There was just something else I needed to do before I went home. Can we do this maybe next week?"

"Babe, all of the guys are bringing their wives, and I don't want to be the only one there without mine. Can you please do me this favor just this once? I'll make it up to you later."

I have to look at the phone for a second to make sure I heard him correctly. I start to tell him to take one of those desperate floozies from his office, since they want to be me so bad anyway.

How many nights have I asked him to join me with colleagues and he told me he couldn't make it? Did I snap out when I found out that he took the little secretary bitch to Chicago for the Society of Hospital Medicine Convention? She might have been taking notes, but they surely weren't about the miracles of modern medicine. I made sure she found out what the inside of the unemployment office looked like shortly after that.

I want to go there, but he has been trying lately to act right, so I guess I could do this for him just once. Besides, Jaydah is still in war mode, so it'd probably be better to deal with her in a few days. As long as we converse before the party, I'll be cool.

"Ray, what time are you talking? I still have five more patients here," I say, trying not to sound annoyed.

"Is eight good? That'll give us all time to meet up at the restaurant without having to rush."

"Eight is fine. I'll meet you there," I say, ready to end the call.

I swear I don't feel like being around the stuck-up wives of his friends. Hell, they act like they are the only ones who have a doctor on their arm. Shit, I have one up, because mine holds the title of Chief of Gynecology.

"Actually, if you don't mind, I'll come get you, so we can ride in the same car. Go home and put on something sexy, and I'll meet you there. That way we don't have to pay valet to park two cars."

"Okay, Ray. Anything else?"

"No, baby, that's it. I love you," he says into the phone, sounding satisfied.

I feel the total opposite and am annoyed by the entire situation. He rarely ever says the word *love* to me, and I don't know what kind of shit he's on now, but I'm not feeling it.

"See you at home," I respond, not even bothering to tell him I loved him back.

Shit, we're moving too damn fast. You don't go from years of barely speaking to being all in love and shit all of a sudden. Now don't get me wrong, because I do love my husband, but let's keep it real. We haven't been this close, and he hasn't been this attentive in never. You've got to break me in slowly. I stay guarded, because who knows when he will be back to the same old Ray Hunter again?

I take my time with the rest of my patients, purposely trying to run late so I won't have to go, but to my dismay I am done and out the door by six-thirty. On the drive home I think briefly about what I should put on, but I can't get Jaydah off my mind. When I get home my husband's 2007 Phantom Drophead Coupe 100EX is parked in front of the door in our circular driveway. I drive my car past his and park farther to the side, so I can drive right out in the morning.

When I walk in the house, I can hear my husband singing off-key to "Sexual Healing" by Marvin Gaye in the kitchen. I stick my head in to let him know I'm home, then I run upstairs to change. In the middle of stripping, I see my husband walk up and stand in the bedroom door. He doesn't say anything; he just watches me while I pull an outfit together and get dressed again. I can tell he wants to get into something, but it's already seven-fifteen by then and we had to be at the restaurant at eight.

When I'm done getting dressed and putting on a little

makeup, he reaches out for my hand, and we leave the house. When we get out to the car, he pushes me up against it and kisses me, slipping his hand under my skirt and using his fingers to pull my thong to the side and finger my clit before he opens the door for me to get in.

I have to blink my eyes and shake my head to get it together because this is definitely a new man I am dealing with. He has a sly smile on his face when he gets into the car, and he says nothing as he flashes the key card across the sensor and races out of the driveway.

Within a half hour we are at the restaurant waiting for the valet to park his car.

Once valet arrives, Ray comes around to my side of the car, extending his hand to help me out. My pussy feels slippery, and I can feel my clit pressed against the soft fabric of my thong, causing my legs to buckle a little after I get out. He softly kisses me again before we get into the restaurant, and we're immediately seated. His colleagues are already there, enjoying glasses of champagne.

I smile and speak to everyone at the table, keeping up the appearance of being a happy couple. All of the men speak back, their eyes freely roaming my body, hoping to see an erect nipple or something like that. Their wives, however, give me snooty hellos and turned their noses up at me. I could care less. They're just mad because I have a banging body, and it wasn't due to multiple plastic surgeries.

My husband takes his seat next to me, and we all converse between ordering appetizers and entrées. I hear someone ask my husband when he will have a little Ray or Midori running around, and I don't quite hear his answer because at that very moment Jaydah walks into the restaurant with a drop-dead gorgeous woman on her arm.

I struggle to keep a straight face as we make eye contact before she is seated at a table not too far from the one we occupy. I'm pissed! How could she be with someone else that soon? We didn't even get a chance to talk.

I half pay attention to the conversation at the table, occasionally nodding and throwing in a laugh or giggle. Jaydah is sitting facing me, looking me dead in my eyes. I want to go over there so bad, but I can't. I hope Ray doesn't notice her sitting there, but my luck runs out as quickly as that thought pops into my head.

"Honey, scoot back a little. I want to go use the restroom before our food is served."

I move my chair over to give him room, and just my luck, he heads right in Jaydah's direction. When he gets closer to the table, he almost makes it past without noticing her, but she reaches out and grabs his arm, stopping him in mid-stride. I can see them talking, and she introduces him to the woman she's with. My prayers then turn into him not bringing her over, but God be doing something else, because He is not hearing me this evening.

I see her get up, and the next thing you know, he is bringing her over to our table, introducing her to everyone seated. I'm cool with that, as long as we keep it brief, but when he offers for them to come join us, I almost lose it.

The men at the table agree, but the women have the same look on their face as I do. The waiter doesn't waste any time setting up their chairs right next to me and my husband, and I feel sick instantly when Jaydah sits down right next to me.

"Hi, nice to see you again. I didn't quite catch your name the last time we met. What was it again?"

"Midori," I say through clenched teeth, wanting to punch her in her damn neck. I can't believe she's acting like this.

"Midori . . . my favorite drink. I'm Jaydah, nice to meet you again. This is my date, Nevaeh. She models for Ford Models."

I look at my husband to see if he had caught the slip-up, because when he and Jaydah initially met she told him her name was Sarah. But he acts like it didn't faze him in the least.

The men are like panting dogs waiting to jump on a damn bone. A closer look at Nevaeh makes me remember seeing her face on the cover of *King* magazine back in December.

I can't believe the turn this evening has taken. And to think I was concerned about her being in the house all alone. I guess my husband didn't have to go to the bathroom after all, because he sits back down.

I try to enjoy my meal, but I am screaming on the inside. All the fake smiling and forced conversation is giving me a damn headache. I want this night to end as soon as possible, and hopefully I'll make it through without snapping the hell out.

You Must Not Know 'Bout Me

Jaydah

I laughed all the way through dinner. It's funny how shit comes together because when I called Nevaeh I was trying to get my mind off Midori. I'm not even going to hold you. I was scheming, trying to think of a way to rub that shit in her face, and to my surprise, I was able to do just that.

Nevaeh is absolutely beautiful, with kissable lips, a fat ass, and curves in all the right places. She kind of puts you in the mind of Hoopz from the *Flavor of Love* reality show. I had to show her off before we got into something. It turned me on that everywhere we went, men fell all over her, not knowing that they didn't have a snowball's chance in hell of taking her home. She let me do whatever I wanted to do to her, and it was so easy to make her cum. She made sure it was worth her while being with me whenever she came through.

On the flip side of that, we never worked out because we were too much alike. She demanded too much of my attention, and wasn't understanding of the fact that I had deadlines to meet. I was just supposed to be cool with her running around all crazy, doing photo shoots and shit, but when I was trying to push out an eighty-thousand-word manuscript she couldn't understand that I needed some alone time.

With that aside, we were in the right place at the right time to make Midori miserable. It was funny running into them because I was just commenting on the car that was parked in front of mine waiting for valet to move it. I kept saying that I had seen it somewhere, and as soon as I walked into the restaurant and saw Midori, I knew it would be on.

She looked extra uncomfortable, and I was enjoying it a little too much. I mean, shit, I showed her that I loved her unconditionally, and this is how it ends up for me? Her husband was making me sick too, with his corny ass, but he would prove to be useful later on. I just had to figure out how I would use him to my benefit.

When Nevaeh and I got home that night, I tore that ass up, but I couldn't even look at her because all I kept seeing was Midori. My mind drifted, and I pictured it was Midori lying there instead of Nevaeh. I treated her body just like I did with Midori, taking her nipples into my mouth and swirling my tongue around them until her body started to tremble. She had her legs wrapped around my waist, since we were both sitting up in the bed, and I used the small electric vibrator she liked so much to stimulate her clit.

She had the "butterfly" inside of her, and I held the controller in my hand, switching the speed from low to high simultaneously. She was squirming on top of me and moaning in my ear, and that shit had me ready to cum. I almost said Midori's name out loud, but I caught myself. Nevaeh was so into it, I don't think she would have noticed.

But I wanted to get this done and over with. Pressing her clit between my thumb and forefinger, and turning the butterfly on high had her going into convulsions, and before long, she was depositing a sticky puddle on my sheets.

We showered and got into bed afterward, and before I knew it, it was morning. She didn't stick around, saying that she had a show to do in Paris, and that she had to get home and pack. I acted like I didn't want her to go, but I was relieved she was rolling out. Maybe I could actually get some work done.

It's been three days since that entire restaurant incident, and Midori has been ringing my phone off the hook. I didn't bother to answer either phone, and by the third day I had turned the ringer off on my home phone, and my cell phone was completely off, forwarding my messages straight to voice mail. I would check my messages periodically, and the only calls I returned were to my publicist and to my publisher, the CEO of Hot Topicz Publications.

I'm still trying to decide if I'm going to buy her a birthday gift or not. What I should do is take her all the shit I bought her for Valentine's Day instead. I bet her husband doesn't know she has a fetish for vibrators. I swear I don't feel like being stressed out right now, but every time I think about that shit I get mad.

I already have my outfit picked out. I got a cute little black Juicy Couture mini dress with silver-and-black stiletto open-toe heels to match. I'll be topping it off with silver accessories, and I'll probably get my hair pulled up off my neck somehow. Either way, I'll make sure I'm noticed when I walk up in there, and Midori will wish she had brought her ass over here like she was supposed to.

I had forty-two missed calls from her over the last three days and about twenty-seven messages, starting with her apologizing, and ending with her cursing me out. I'm sure she's just scared I am going to say some shit to her husband, but her secrets are safe with me. She will learn not to make promises she can't keep after this, though. I guarantee you that.

February 22, 2007

Midori

Jaydah wouldn't answer any of my calls. I have been calling her since the night we left the restaurant, trying to talk to her. It was an awkward evening, to say the least, but I survived. I wanted to touch base with her before she showed up at my party. I know there isn't any sense in trying to talk her out of coming at this point, but maybe if I could offer her something to diffuse the situation a little she might just act right. Most importantly, I want to know who the hell that woman was who was with her. Was she my replacement?

I should have been a damn actress because Lord knows I gave an award-winning performance at that table, but in reality I was ready to snap out. I really couldn't hear what anyone was saying. I was annoyed at Jaydah and this Nevaeh bitch, and Ray kept rubbing my stomach like we already had a child on the way. I have never been that irritated in my life, and if Jaydah had said that Nevaeh was *heaven* spelled backwards one more time, I would have went the hell off.

Jaydah and Ray together that up close and personal was too much going on at one time.

When I come down the stairs, the hired help is putting the finishing touches on the party decorations. Ray had all of the furniture in the dining room moved upstairs so the room can be used for dancing. The French doors opened to our indoor pool area, where all of the refreshments and drinks will be serviced, since it's too cold to be outside. We won't be doing a traditional sit-down dinner for the party, just hors d'oeuvres, such as wings, caviar, and finger sandwiches.

The decorations are absolutely beautiful. There are streamers and balloons hanging up around the room in silver, gold, and black to match the silk tablecloths and gold centerpieces. A gold fountain spewing rum punch sits to the side, and the lights in the pool will be turned on later tonight. Everything is perfect, and the smells from the food cooking in the kitchen remind me that I'm hungry. I have to fit into my dress later on, though, so I won't be eating too much.

After a small breakfast and a quick shower, I follow the schedule that Ray had set up for me for today. He gives me an all-day spa treatment as one of my birthday gifts every year, and I will be getting my hair and nails done from the stylist team he has coming to the house later on tonight. When I go outside to get into my car, there is a limo waiting for me in the driveway to take me everywhere I need to go.

I am so surprised, and when I turned to get Ray he is standing at the top of the steps, smiling down at me. Even though Ray and I don't have a romantic type of relationship, he always goes out of his way to make my birthday a special day for me, which is part of the reason why I lied to Jaydah about when I was born. I couldn't take this day from him even if I wanted to.

"Happy birthday, baby." Ray smiles at me from the top of the steps.

"Ray, everything is coming together so nicely. I love you," I say before I realize what I'm saying. I hadn't uttered those words to him in years, and he rarely told me he loved me, so I just keep it moving.

"I love you too, baby. Now get going. You have a schedule you need to keep."

We kiss, and then he opens the car door for me to get in. I sit back in the seat and pour myself a glass of champagne, still shocked at our exchange of affection. *I love you.* Three simple words that I have probably said to Jaydah a million times over the last two years. The funny thing is, I am not a hundred percent sure that I actually do love her. I mean, I care a lot about her, but love? Now, I'm not so sure. I love the things she does to my body, but I can't honestly say she has my heart. Lately, I'm starting to think that my husband still has it in the palm of his hands, and I have forgotten about it.

The limo pulls up to the spa center a half hour later, where the woman who would be doing my massage greets me. I'm glad it's a woman and not a man because they tend to be too rough.

I do as I am instructed and remove all of my clothes and wrap myself in a fluffy bathrobe. The masseuse tells me to get up on the table after she begins playing a tape with slow music.

I close my eyes when her soft hands make contact with my back, and she rubs warm oil into my skin.

* * *

I close my eyes tighter and pretend I am back at Jaydah's condo the first night we decided we would make love. By that time we had been hanging out for a few weeks, flirting with each other and all that. It was raining outside, and I remember being pissed at Ray about some shit that happened the previous evening.

"Take off your clothes and lay across the bed. I'll give you a massage," Jaydah said almost innocently while she got up to get her massage oil out of the hall closet.

I was hesitant at first, but I quickly stripped down to my thong and lay on my stomach so my breasts would be covered.

She came back to the room in a thong also, and lust was written all over her face. She started at my feet and worked every knot out of my tired body. Pretty soon, all thoughts of Ray and how much he pissed me off were erased from my mind, and the feeling of her warm hands running up and down my body made me feel at ease.

She had a firm yet gentle grip that made my tense muscles melt like butter in her hands. I tensed up a little when I felt her hands rub across my bare ass, and when her thumb grazed the lips of my pussy, my walls began to pulsate. I said I was not going to go there with her, but my body was betraying me, producing a sticky sweetness that made my thong stick to my body.

Umm . . . maybe we should stop. I realized that thought didn't reach my lips when I heard a moan instead.

Jaydah took the initiative and spread my legs, taking post in between them. She massaged the insides of my thighs, her fingers teasing the space in between the lips of my pussy and where the insides of my thighs connected.

I stretched my arms out in front of me and placed my head into the pillow to muffle my scream. I wanted to feel something in me, now!

This wasn't my first time being with a woman. There was just something about a woman knowing what she was doing that turned me the hell on. Before I met Ray, I did the girl-on-girl thing plenty of times, but when I really got into my career and met him, I put all of that wild mess to the side . . . until I met Jaydah. Now look at me.

As the masseuse continues to work the stress from my body, I daydream about how Jaydah's lips felt pressed against my lips. She had nice full lips and a long tongue that worked magic. She would press her closed mouth against me first, kissing me as if she was kissing the lips on my face. I would spread my legs open, so she could have easy access to what she enjoyed the most. With her lips still closed, she would stick her tongue out, and it felt like it wrapped around my clit on contact. She used her hands to support my back and would squeeze my ass cheeks, causing my lips to open wider.

"Are you enjoying your massage, Mrs. Hunter?" the masseuse whispered in my ear. For a second, she sounded like Jaydah.

"Yes, please don't stop."

I remember her taking my clit into her mouth and humming against it, sending me into convulsions. Jaydah had a way of bringing forth orgasms that made you look like the demon from *The Exorcist* had crawled up in you. I have to press my mouth in the towel to control my orgasm and keep from moaning out loud while getting my massage.

Just when I think I'm going to explode, the masseuse is done, and I get up with a flushed face and wobbly legs so I can get my clothes back on. Shit, I'm almost embarrassed, and I give her an extra nice tip for bringing back such fond memories.

Back inside the limo, I talk to Ray briefly before pulling up to Cache to pick up my dress. It's a sexy black tube dress that flares out from the waist and has a semi-train in the back. Silver jewelry from Tiffany's and strappy sandals will complete my outfit. I plan to wear my hair in an up-do, and French on my fingers and toes. Simple, yet elegant.

When I arrive back home all of the decorations are up, the ice sculptures have arrived, and the food smells delicious. When I get up to the room, Ray is lying in the bed knocked out, looking so at peace. I set my bag on the dresser before taking a seat next to him on the bed. The styling team will be here within an hour, and I want to already be showered so my hair won't fall from the steam.

The weight of my body on the bed makes Ray open his eyes, and once he is focused, he smiles at me and pulls me over to lie next to him. I make myself comfortable, resting my head on his shoulder and closing my eyes.

"How was your massage?" he asks, his voice still a little groggy from his nap.

"Everything was wonderful," I say, smiling up at him. A little guilt begins to creep in because, when I should have been thinking about him, I was thinking about Jaydah.

"Good, the girls should be here to do your hair shortly."

"Thanks so much for this, Ray. I really appreciate all of this."

"Thank you for being my wife. I know we've grown apart over the last few years, but I want us to get back tight again. I miss us."

I don't even have a comeback for that. A part of me gets a little salty because if it weren't for him running around on me with those office bitches we wouldn't even be having this conversation. That's why I turned to Jaydah for comfort, and now I'm scared that I won't be able to let her go.

Instead of responding, I use my free hand to loosen up his pants and take hold of his dick. It wasn't like he was a Mandingo warrior or anything like that, but he has enough for me to deep-throat without gagging.

He closes his eyes and moans when my warm hand makes contact with his dick, and when I stroke him up and down he gets hard instantly.

I move from my spot beside him, and get on my knees beside him in the bed.

He looks at me through half-closed eyes, and I give him something to look at. Pulling him through the slit in his boxers, I take all of him in my mouth and slurp and suck on him the way he likes it. He holds the back of my neck and fucks my mouth slow, yet urgently, and I am taking that shit like a pro.

With one hand I play with his balls and I use the other to pinch his nipples, until I could taste his eruption in the back of my throat. I suck on him until his shaking subsides and his dick goes limp.

Just as I lean up, one of the helpers knocks on the bedroom door to let us know the stylist has arrived. I don't say a word. I just strip naked and hop in the shower, donning a bathrobe so I won't mess up my clothes. I have my game face on, and I'm ready to get this party started!

Any Time, Any Place

Jaydah

I walk up in that bitch like I own the joint. When I pull up to the crib in my brand-new butterscotch 2007 Maxima with the Reese's Cup interior, valet thinks I'm a fuckin' celebrity, and I feel like one. All eyes are on me as I strut up the stairs and into the Hunter household, and I am eating the attention up. Men are practically drooling on their tuxedo jackets, and their women have their faces frowned up because they wish they had a body like mine. I don't see Midori immediately, but I make sure I am noticed as I stand in the middle of the foyer and look from left to right.

The deejay is killing it on the ones and twos, easing one of my concerns, because I thought I would have to be listening to elevator music while watching these square-ass doctors dance off-beat for the entire night. To my surprise, 50 Cent is blaring from the speakers, and quite a few folks are getting it on on the dance floor.

I haven't even been here for a good five minutes and already I have had to turn down a good six invitations to dance. I don't want Midori to notice me right away, and shaking my ass on the dance floor would definitely draw attention. I walk over to the fountain, where a handsome waiter offers me a drink. I take it as a means of having something to do with my hands while I scout the scene for either Midori or Ray to make an entrance.

She doesn't disappoint me in the least. Within five minutes Ray calls for everyone's attention so the birthday girl can make her entrance. I'm speechless as I watch Midori emerge at the top of the stairs. She looks stunning in a black dress similar to the one I'm wearing, and I get wet instantly, picturing her without any panties on underneath, or maybe just a thong.

I take a gulp of my drink to keep from moaning out loud, and as applause rises around the room, I dip farther to the back of the room, so she won't see me right away. I'm not ready to see her face to face, because I am still a little mad at her. I ain't gonna hold you, though. If I could just taste her one more time, I'd forgive her for all the shit we just went through.

As she makes her rounds toward where I'm hiding out, I make my way in the other direction, dipping around people, snaking around the tables, until I get back to the foyer entrance.

I thought I had gotten by scot-free, but I hear Ray call my name out. I pause for a second, but reluctantly turn around. He is walking toward me with a man beside him, both of them dripping with lust.

"Jaydah, I am so glad you made it. Tell me you're not leaving already," he says in a sincere voice, but his eyes make contact with everything but my face. His friend's eyes explore my body in the same fashion.

I am almost tempted to turn around so they can get a back view. "No, I wasn't leaving just yet. I left Midori's gift in my car, and I was going out to get it. I was going to sit it with the others," I reply with a fake smile that neither notice because their eyes are fixated on my breasts. I didn't tell a complete lie, though. Midori's gift was in my car, but I was trying to keep from running into her so soon.

"Oh, don't worry about that now. She won't be opening up gifts until eleven forty-three tonight. That was the actual time she was born," he says with a look of satisfaction on his face.

I keep the same fake smile plastered on mine.

"Here she comes now," his partner says, still never taking his eyes from my body.

I'm sure he has a wife here who would slap him up for staring so hard, but if he didn't care, why should I?

Ray turns in the direction his wife is coming, calling her over to where we are standing. The smile on my face is replaced with a smirk as she gets closer, my eyes saying it all.

She was smiling widely and chatting it up, until she noticed me standing there. She gives Ray a passionate kiss on his mouth that turns my stomach completely, but I hold it down. All of a sudden they're in love, and I wasn't feeling that shit at all.

"Honey, you remember Jaydah, right? Actually, Darren, this is Jaydah," he says, finally introducing me to his friend. "He's the top pathologist at the hospital. Jaydah is a—what do you do again, Jaydah?"

My entire face must have gotten flush red. Ray knows damn well we had never even discussed that before now. Not even at dinner, where all of the conversation was about him and his colleagues. I play it smooth, though.

He obviously doesn't know who he's fucking with. Midori has an embarrassed look on her face, but that doesn't bother me in the least. She doesn't have a reason to be embarrassed—not yet.

"I am a best-selling novelist," I reply snidely, letting him know that he really didn't want to battle.

"Oh, are you now? I read a lot. What are the names of some of your works?" Darren chimes in, finally making eye contact.

Midori responds before I have a chance to talk. "Darren, your wife has her book. You remember the one we were reading about the married couple and that crazy woman who was trying to break them up?" she asks, desperately trying to diffuse the situation.

"Oh, yeah, I do. That chick was crazy. There will be no threesomes for me," he says, laughing at his own joke.

I thank Midori in my head for getting me out of that one, but she still has some shit with her.

"Okay, well, do any of you want to dance?" Midori asks as the beat from "Chicken Noodle Soup" by Webstar comes over the speakers.

This would be hilarious watching a bunch of grown-ass people trying to do that dance.

"Yes, please, let's dance. Darren, bring Jaydah out on this dance floor and let's get it crunk," Ray says, dragging us out to the middle of the floor.

They are really letting their hair down up in here, because I'm sure they're a bunch of stuffed shirts in their everyday lives.

I am hesitant at first because I don't want this guy's wife to come running up on me, but I begin to loosen up and get my party on with the rest of the crowd as the deejay drops one hot track after another.

When Fat Joe starts making it rain on his hot new track, money starts falling from the ceiling. I grab at one of the bills floating in front of me, and it is a hundred-dollar bill with Midori's face on it in place of the president's. On the back of it is a thank you for helping Midori celebrate her birthday. Outside of those few alterations it looks like real money. Ray had definitely gone all out for this party.

We're jamming hard up in here while getting our drink on, and on a few occasions Midori and I dance together as a crowd forms around us. We bump and grind to Lil Mama's hit song "Lip Gloss," and it makes me horny as shit because I haven't been this close to her in weeks. This song was one I had heard down South first, but it won't be until the spring when Philly catches on. We laugh and smile and enjoy the party, and pretty soon it's time for Midori to open her gifts.

I have one of the valet workers bring mine in, and I stand in the cut to watch her open her stuff. She gets everything, from diamond bracelets from Asha, to fur coats and gift cards to some of her favorite stores. When she gets to my gift I know she'll blush because it's more personal. I would have preferred her open her gifts at my condo so we can enjoy them in private, but for now I will conform. I have a new toy for her, but that's back at the crib. I didn't think it would be appropriate for this type of setting, but the champagne-colored nightie she pulls from the box with six-inch heels to match are right up her alley.

"Looks like we'll be getting that little Midori or Ray sooner than we thought," someone says from the crowd, drawing a quick laugh from the spectators.

I for one don't find it funny, but I let it slide.

She continues to open her gifts, and when she's done, Ray stacks them neatly on the table for the guests to admire.

The deejay turns the music back up, and it's on again. I'm standing to the side, watching everyone dance and have a good time, when Midori walks up and glues her body to the side of mine. I don't know what this is about, or if she has been drinking, but I know she doesn't want her husband to see us hugged up in this atmosphere.

"Walk with me to the back. I want to show you my husband's car collection."

I don't say a word. I simply turn toward the direction she is already walking in, and follow her to the back of the house.

She takes me to a room that is down in the back of their finished basement that houses five cars, including a vintage 1940 Mercedes Benz. We walk toward the front of the room (which looks more like a garage).

Once she turns the lights on, she gets up on the hood of the car.

"So, you still upset with me?" she asks with a glassy look in her eyes, indicating and confirming that she is tore the hell up.

I guess all of those Midori sours are starting to kick in.

"Of course, I am, Midori. You lied to me," I respond, trying not to pay attention to the fact that my assumption was right.

She is leaned back on the hood of the car with her legs spread open, showing me her bare pussy. It turns me on that she doesn't have any panties on under her dress. We were way too much alike.

"I'll make it up to you. As a matter of fact," she says, spreading the lips of her juicy pussy and sliding a finger in, tasting it afterwards, "come and show me what I've been missing."

I'm a little hesitant at first because I don't want her to think she has me like that, but I can't resist tasting her on my tongue. I walk over and stand in front of her, opening her up with my thumb and forefinger, examining her from my position at the head of the car. I can feel her pulsating on my fingertips, and I think briefly about messing up my dress before I lean over to taste her. I know I give in too easily, but I can't help it. It's like her pussy and my tongue are magnets.

I feel like it'd been forever, as my tongue melts into her soft folds and her juice covers my lips, tasting sweet like candy. My moans match hers as I devour her body, causing her to cum back to back.

It feels good being with her like this, but I know eventually Ray will come to look for her. And as soon as I stand up, he appears in the doorway. Midori had just pulled her dress down, and I am wiping her essence off of my chin with a party napkin.

"Honey, here you are. I was looking all over for you. Dr. Robinson has started a Soul Train line, and we need you to come pop, lock, and drop it," he says with a bright smile on his face, obviously enjoying himself.

"Oh, I was just showing Jaydah your car collection. We'll be right there," she says to him.

Obviously her answer is good enough, because he turns and goes back to the party, seemingly suspecting nothing.

"Do you have a bathroom nearby?" I ask her, feeling awkward about what just went down.

"Yes, you can use the one in my room, and no one will see you. The towels are in the linen closet behind the bathroom door. I'll be at your house tomorrow to finish this off."

I don't even take what she said for face value, since I'm already pissed at myself for falling for her ass—again. She makes her way to the dance floor, and I go upstairs to find the restroom so I can clean myself up.

Once done, I don't even bother to stay. I have valet bring my car around and I jet, opting to go work on my book that's due shortly, and get ready for Midori to stop by tomorrow. I can't wait to test out our new toy.

Going In Circles

Midori

My head is pounding like I got my ass beat last night. I can't even remember coming up to the room, but I remember the party being off the chain and ending at like four in the morning. Once we got everyone out, Ray and I made use of some of that cake icing and the sturdiness of the kitchen table. He was dicking me down something serious, and I remember crawling toward the steps, but everything else is a blank. It must have been good, because my pussy is sore as hell and I got cake icing in my damn hair.

I didn't forget Jaydah's presence at the party, though. I let her go down on me last night, and I'm almost certain I opened up a new can of worms. I probably promised her we'd work it out and all that, but the bottom line is Jaydah and I just can't be. There is too much at stake, and I am not willing to risk it all any longer. Ray is acting right for now, so that's what I am focusing on.

It's two in the afternoon, so I know she's probably

called me at least a hundred times, but my phone was on the dresser, and I couldn't lift my head off the pillow to get it. I don't know where Ray is, and I don't have the strength to call out for him. Luckily for me, he walks into the room a few minutes later.

"Looks like someone enjoyed their birthday, huh?" Ray says, sitting the tray he was carrying on the nightstand.

It appears that he made me breakfast, but all I have a taste for is a couple of Excedrin and a cup of coffee to knock off this hangover.

I manage to lift my head from the pillow and sit up so he can put the serving tray on my lap. The room feels like it's spinning, and I almost vomit on the tray. Moving it quickly, I jump up and sprint toward the bathroom, barely making the toilet as yesterday's food and alcohol burns my throat, splashing water in my face as it makes contact with the inside of the toilet bowl.

Ray comes into the bathroom behind me, helping me wipe my mouth and holding my hair back for me.

Then yesterday comes rushing up again. *Damn, I feel like shit.*

After about twenty minutes of dry heaving I get my shit together enough to crawl back to the bed. What the hell did I eat last night? Ray is worried, and offers to call out, but I tell him to go ahead and get to work. I just have to get my head together. Thankfully, I don't have to go into the office today.

Around four, I finally start feeling a little better, so I get up to see how many calls I've missed. My parents and my sister left me messages wishing me a happy birthday, and my mom mentioned coming to visit in a few weeks because they couldn't make it up from Norfolk for my party. My brother sent me a video message from him and his family with birthday greetings and said that they would be stopping by soon, too. That made me smile, but when I see that I had a shitload of missed calls and most of them were from Jaydah, my entire attitude changes. It's crazy because she didn't leave a message, which was unusual for her, and that scares me even more. It wasn't in my plan, but if I do nothing else today I'll have to stop by her spot.

Deciding to get it done with as soon as possible, I go ahead and hop in the shower, mad as hell because I have to wash my hair to get the cake icing out. The stylist team Ray hired did a wonderful job, and now I am washing it all down the drain.

I come from the shower to a ringing phone, and when I see that it's Jaydah calling again I ignore the call. I'll just deal with her when I get there.

It doesn't take me long to get it together, and before I leave the house, I call Ray to let him know I am okay and that I will be going out for a while. On my way out I grab a piece of toast and some coffee from the breakfast tray Ray brought up for me, and I am glad to see that the cleaning service we hired is putting my house back in order. After the festivities were over, it was way too much for me and Ray to try to get the place back in order by ourselves.

Forty-five minutes later I pull up to Jaydah's condo. I sit in my car for a half hour, going back on forth on whether I should go in or not. I decide that the least I can do is give her some closure. I care about her, and I would hope that we can at least still be cool. At the very least, all she could do is dismiss me from her life.

One thing I keep repeating while I walk up to her door is that I am not going to give in and have sex with her. This meeting is about closure, nothing else.

I ring the bell, and within seconds Jaydah is at the door. Her eyes are bloodshot with heavy bags under them like she has been in tears all day. Knowing Jaydah, she probably was. She's always been a damn crybaby. I don't really know what to say, and she saves me the embarrassment by just walking away and leaving the door open.

When I walk in I see that she is burning candles, and there is a gift box sitting on the kitchen table. It is a pleasant surprise, considering that she gave me a gift yesterday, but I ignore it, opting to cater to her instead. She is stretched out on her bed in a cute little silk kimono, and she is typing away on her laptop. I really feel bad at that moment because she had already told me that her next book was almost due, and here I am causing all kinds of mental blockage.

I sit next to her on the bed, and surprisingly she moves over so we don't make contact.

"What are you doing?" I ask, trying to get a feel on how much attitude she has. Shit, after I tell her we are through, she probably won't have much rap for me anyway.

"I have an interview in the morning on *The Steve Harvey Morning Show,* and I was going over some interview questions my publicist sent over yesterday," she says, not looking up from the screen.

"*The Steve Harvey Morning Show?* That is great. I listen to him every morning!"

I was so excited for Jaydah. In only two short years she's managed to put out two novels, participate in five collaborations with other authors, and has made several best-seller lists. That's a lot for an author to accomplish in that small amount of time, and she is truly getting the recognition she deserves.

"I know that, and when I told you about it a month ago, you told me you would go to New York with me for the interview. Guess you forgot," she shoots back nonchalantly, like she doesn't even care anymore.

It's funny, because I remember that clear as day, and I sure did tell her I would go.

"Jaydah, I am so sorry. I totally forgot. I could still go," I plead with her, forgetting that I came over here to end it with her for good.

"Don't worry about it. I called Nevaeh this morning, and she was more than willing to go down on—I mean, go down there with me. I get a copy of the tape though, so I'll make you one if you'd like." She never takes her face from the screen. After that remark I am ready to fuck her up in here. I know she just didn't throw that Nevaeh bitch in my face, like I should feel threatened. Shit, I have a husband at home, I don't need this shit, but I'll be damned if I will be replaced, especially by some wannabe model bitch.

"Jaydah, I said I would go." I come back with a lot more attitude in my voice this time around. It is enough to make her turn and look my way.

"I'm leaving at five in the morning, and I'm not coming back until Tuesday evening. If you want to go, be here on time or be left."

I'm shocked to say the least, but at this point, I am prepared to do anything. I can't believe the turn we've taken, and it isn't for the better.

She turns her attention back to the task she was handling, and I get up to go home. She doesn't even budge, and this is so unlike the Jaydah I know. Any other time she would beg me to stay, but today she doesn't seem to care. Maybe she's fed up.

When I get to the door, I am hoping she would say something, but she doesn't. I turn back around and look at her. I walk back over to her and snatched the laptop from under her. She is going to pay attention to me whether she wants to or not.

What bothers me even more is that she doesn't even react. She just smiles and turns over on her back so she could look at me.

"What the fuck is your problem?" I ask her after putting the laptop on the dresser. She has me so damn confused and frustrated.

"Why do you think I have a problem?" Jaydah asks with the same nonchalant attitude she's had since I'd gotten here, really pissing me off.

"You sitting here acting all stank, like you don't give a damn whether I'm here or not."

"Midori, I'm not acting any different than I did yester-day. Didn't you always say that I need to respect the fact that you have a husband? Well, that's what I'm doing."

"And since when did you listen to me? You pop up at my house unannounced, you crash my damn party—"

"Correction, I was invited to your party."

"After you popped up at my damn house! You know what, I'm tired of this shit," I say as I storm toward the door. This bitch is just about working my very last nerve, and I'm ready to hurt her up in here.

When I get to the door and turn the knob, Jaydah laughs out loud, and at that point I am seeing red. I turn around, and she's completely naked and on her knees.

The kimono is now on the floor, and she has a devilish look on her face.

"So, are you mad at me now, Midori? Seems as though you don't like it when the tables are turned," she says as she gets out of the bed and starts walking toward me.

She looks delicious, and I know I can't walk away from her. I just have to find a way to juggle her and Ray—that's what it all boils down to.

When she gets up to me, she presses her naked body against mine and pushes my hair back behind my ear with her soft hands. She smells like the Very Sexy 2 perfume I got her from Victoria's Secret for her birthday last August, and her softness pressed up against me is making me weak.

"You just gonna walk out, huh?" Jaydah whispers in my ear before tonguing my earlobe and pulling it between her teeth.

My pussy starts to pulsate instantly.

"Let me make it up to you."

I don't say another word. I let her lead me to the bed, where she takes her time stripping me and tasting me all over. Why couldn't Ray satisfy me like this *ALL* the time? Jaydah has my head spinning in circles, and I feel like I'm watching the entire scene from across the room. I find my-self falling again, and I know after this it will be murder trying to get away.

Three hours later I leave Jaydah's house on sore legs, and all I can do is soak in the Jacuzzi and get back in bed.

Ray comes home around nine that night, and we have a wonderful dinner that he had arranged as another part of my birthday gift. When I get up to go back upstairs, I walk into my room to see our luggage packed.

"Ray, what's this about?" I ask as I step over the suitcases. He must have had our maid pack the bags while we were eating dinner, but I can't go anywhere. I already promised Jaydah I'd be with her tomorrow.

"There's a limo out front to take us to the airport. Since you don't go back to work until next week, we'll be celebrating your birthday in Belize. I got us a gorgeous suite at the Hamanasi Resort. We can lay back and chill before you get back into working hard."

I don't have time to think before we are whisked away to the airport.

Before I know it we are landing and checking into the resort, and I still haven't had a chance to call Jaydah. I swear every time I take one step forward, I get pushed two steps back.

Big Time

Jaydah

She lied. The funny thing is I expected it and I'm still surprised—a little. I thought for sure after putting that shit on her the way I did last night she would be running to my doorstep bright and early, but I have been calling since five this morning and her phone is going straight to voice mail. I'm due to be in the air at eight o'clock, so by five-thirty I have no choice but to head out without her.

I call Nevaeh once I get to the New Jersey Turnpike, and I meet her in Elizabeth, New Jersey on my way to the Big Apple. Nevaeh may be funny-acting, but she's reliable and I know I will have never had to remind her to be somewhere. There I was trying to find an excuse for her not to go, and I end up needing her. I have definitely got to evaluate who I'm fooling with this year.

It takes everything in me not to call Midori, and even after I stop to pick up Nevaeh I still call her a couple of times, if for nothing else but to curse her ass out, and she still isn't picking up. It's cool, though. She'll see how I turn the tables, and she won't like it, not one bit.

When I get to the radio station I am greeted by the production manager, who in turn introduces me to Carla, Tommy, Shirley, and Steve, the team who make up *The Steve Harvey Morning Show*. They all make me feel comfortable immediately. Even though my publicist had given me a list of questions they might possibly ask, she told me to be prepared for the conversation to switch up and turn at any moment. I'm excited and nervous at the same time, but Nevaeh gave me the energy I needed to make this happen, and pretty soon thoughts of Midori are long gone.

After I am situated in the studio with my headphones on, I flash Nevaeh a quick smile just as the commercial ends, and we get into the interview.

"We're back, ladies and gentlemen, and with us we have the talented *New York Times* best-selling author of *She Belongs to Me* and *Second Time Around*. She has also participated in several collaborations, and is the recipient of the *2006 Writers On The Move Award*. Give it up for Miss Jaydah B.," Steve Harvey says with a warm smile on his face, instantly making me feel at ease.

"Thank you so much for having me. I'm so happy to be here," I reply, smiling shyly and still not believing I've made it this far.

"Look at her trying to act like she shy, unc. Boy, if she was a little thicker—"

"Tommy, stop embarrassing the woman. Can't you see she's over here shaking?" Shirley says jokingly, reprimanding Tommy and bringing laughter from all of us in the room.

"I'm cool, Shirley. I have to bat off men like Tommy all the time."

"And I know that's right, with your fine self. If you was just a little older, I would just—"

"Steve, act like we're on nationally syndicated radio," Carla joins in the conversation, drawing another round of laughter. "Jaydah, start by telling us how you came to be on top."

"I got this, Carla," Steve says, pretending like he has an attitude.

The energy in the studio has us on fire, and I'm loving it. Shirley rolls her eyes, and Tommy starts panting like he was having a hard time breathing, which makes us all laugh again.

"Miss Jaydah B., please tell us how you got to where you are today. How did you come to meet Nathan Jones, CEO of Hot Topicz Publications?"

"Well, I met Nathan at an issues party I threw at my house back in the summer of 2004. My publicist and long-time friend Talia Skyy brought him over to the house after he was done with some business and signings he had in the Philadelphia area, him originally being from Jamaica, Queens, New York," I say, reminiscing on how I got into the publishing game.

"An issues party? Lord knows we all got issues," Tommy comes in from the sideline, making us laugh. "So you're telling me that all of y'all got together and had a party about having issues?"

"Something like that," I respond, laughing at Tommy's antics. I then break down how the issues party worked.

"What we basically did was write down a bunch of issues and topics, covering everything from sex to baby momma drama, and dropped them into a punch bowl. Once we got started, we pulled the questions out one at time, reading them out loud, and gave everyone a chance to answer. It was usually a mixed crowd of men and women, gay and straight, single and married, so it made for interesting conversation."

"That sounds like something we all need to attend, right after church service," Steve says, cracking his own self up.

I laugh along, really enjoying the interview.

"Okay. So, Jaydah, tell us about your books. From my understanding you have two novels out now, one on the way, and you have done a good amount of collabos that helped get your name out there," Shirley asks, gaining control of the situation.

"*Collabos?* What? She a rapper now? She got something out with Jay-Z and Fiddy?" Tommy asks, clowning me.

"No, Tommy. Collabos, in the book world, are just like those in rap and R&B where several authors get together and write about the same topic."

"See here, that sounds like something Sister Odell know something about," Carla replies, referring to one of Steve's alter egos. Sister Odell is an older church-going woman who knows how to put you right in your place.

"That's correct, Shirley. I've participated in five collaborations, all of which are available nationwide. As for my novels, the first one is about a husband and wife who are having bedroom issues and the husband somehow convinces his wife that if they had a threesome it would fix their problem. Needless to say, that's not how it turns out. That's where all the drama unfolds. The sequel deals with how they handled it all after their lives fell apart, and they are trying to see if they can put it all back together."

"From what I understand about the book, young lady, is that the mistress in the book comes in and tries to take the wife from her husband," Steve says in his Sister Odell character.

"Yes, that's exactly what happens," I reply, nervous about what is going to happen next.

"How much of this story is true, young lady? You know an awful lot to look so innocent," Sister Odell says, drawing laughter from the room once more.

"All of it is strictly fiction, although I get a lot of readers who think I am telling my life story. I'm not into women. Melissa is just a character I made up to go along with the story," I reply to Steve, taking a quick glance at Nevaeh to see her reaction. She has a straight face, showing no emotion, and I don't know if that is good or bad.

Not that I'm trying to hide or anything, but the world doesn't need to know that much of my business. What I do in the privacy of my own home is just that, and besides all that, I'm not interested in ALL women, just Nevaeh and Midori.

"And Melissa was vicious, you hear me?" Carla chimes in. She goes into some of the scenes in the book, causing all kinds of ruckus in the studio.

The phone lines are on fire, and the producers of the show have wide smiles on their faces.

"We're going to take some calls from the listeners after the break so we can get into exactly how crazy Melissa was, and how much Jaydah B. is hiding from us. If you've read either book or just want information, give us a call at 1-888-29-STEVE. It's thirteen minutes after the hour. We'll be

back with *The Steve Harvey Morning Show* after these messages."

I breathe a sigh of relief as we go into commercial
break. Everyone tells me how well I'm doing, and Nevaeh
flashes me a smile from the studio window, with two thumbs
up, confirming what they said.

Within minutes we're back to the show, taking calls and
just having a good time. Steve is humorous as he interviews me as Roscoe and Tongue Tied, two of his other
voices he does on the radio. I'm in stitches the entire time.
I'm also allowed to be a judge on "Other Idol," the morning show's version of *American Idol,* where contestants call
up on the radio and sing their song of choice for a chance
to win prizes.

"So, before we go, we'd like to thank the extremely sexy,
absolutely talented Jaydah B. for hanging out with us this
morning. Tell our listeners again how they can get a hold
of your books and all that," Steve says as the show comes to
a close.

"All of my books can be found on my website, www.Ask
JaydahB.com. You can also find them on amazon.com as
well as Borders and Barnes & Noble. If you have an account with Black Expressions, my books are available
through there also. Check my website every month for
your chance to win a novelty item. Drawings are held once
a month, and it's all about adult pleasure."

"Adult pleasure, my kind of contest," Tommy says, getting laughs all around the room.

"Okay, that's our show, ladies and gentlemen. God willing, we'll meet here tomorrow. Have a blessed one." Steve
concludes the show, afterward thanking me again for
coming on.

Before I leave, I do a few thirty-second commercial spots for the show, then we all head over to Amy Ruth's for an early brunch, since his show ends at ten in the morning.

I'm on cloud nine for the rest of the morning, and before we get into my car to head back to Jersey, the producer gives me two copies of the show on CD, and we are on our way.

I decide to chill with Nevaeh for a couple of days, just to get my head together. I thought I was past the entire Midori situation, but as soon as we are on our way back, I get mad about it all over again. I use the excuse that I had to stay close because of the *Essence* magazine photo shoot I had in the morning.

I mean, it isn't a total lie. *Essence* did offer to put me up for the night, but I don't want to be alone. I have been number one on their fiction best-seller's list for the past six months, and along with a few other others who maintained their top five spots, we are doing a photo shoot for their tribute to urban fiction writers.

We get to her house about an hour and a half later due to rush-hour traffic coming out of Manhattan. Nevaeh has an immaculate condo in Elizabeth, New Jersey that allows her the luxury of getting back and forth to photo shoots in New York in no time. She wants me to come stay with her, but it is more convenient for me to do business from Philly. I traveled to New York a lot for signings and such, but I also did I lot of business down South, so it is easier for me to be in the middle of both directions. Of course, she doesn't understand all that, and I don't even bother to explain after the first hundred or so times.

Once we're settled we take a nice long bath together, afterward cuddling on the couch to watch some movies. I

am still pissed at Midori. I ain't even gonna hold you on
that. I sneak and call her again while Nevaeh is running
the bath for us, and her phone is still going straight to
voice mail. I just want to curse her ass out one good time
and I'll be straight.

Halfway through the movie Nevaeh says she wants to
talk to me about something. She had mentioned it to me
earlier too, but I was trying to avoid the conversation. See,
she doesn't know about me and Midori. She knows I know
her and Ray, but she doesn't know that she and I are inti-
mate. Nevaeh is the jealous type, and even though we
aren't officially together, she would step to Midori like we
were, and I don't feel like all the drama.

"So, are we going to make it official or not?" Nevaeh
asks through bites of popcorn.

I try to act like I didn't hear her, but she pops me in the
head and asks again.

"Nevaeh, you know we don't work out. With your schedule and mine, we wouldn't be able to connect like we
should," I say, not wanting to tell her how I really feel. I
mean, she's excellent in bed, but otherwise she is a pain
in the ass.

"I understand that you have things to do, and I'm willing to give you room. I know how important your books
are, and I won't bother you. I think you should give us a
chance."

"You say that now, but you know how you get. Remember what happened the last time?"

"I know, and I'm a different person now. Give me a
chance."

I think about it for a while before responding. It ain't
like Midori is ever going to leave Ray. Shit, the way they're

living, she'd be a fool. It's obvious from her not showing up this morning that her loyalty lies with her husband. On the flip side of all that, I know Nevaeh is so extra, and I'm really not in the mood.

"So, you're just going to ignore me, huh?" Nevaeh says like she was hurt.

"Look, let's just see what happens. We can be exclusive, but let's not rush into anything. I don't want to hurt you, and I don't want to be hurt either. Is that fair?"

"I'm cool with that, but for how long?"

"We'll just play it by ear, Nevaeh."

"Okay, but one last question."

I turn to look at her, so she can see the annoyance on my face. This is part of the reason why I don't want to go there with her. I'm making a mistake, and I know it. Later on I'll regret this, I'm sure.

"What's your question?"

"Do you love me?"

"Yes, Nevaeh, I love you."

"Okay, I was just making sure."

Shaking my head, I turn back around to watch the movie, but soon I'm fast asleep. Thoughts of Midori rush through my mind, but I know I have to move on. All we have are memories and bullshit, and I am definitely cool on that.

I will tell you exactly where I was but . . .

Midori

"**Y**ou keep cutting me off."

It isn't until Wednesday afternoon that I finally find a free minute to call Jaydah. She won't let me get a word in edgewise, but that's to be expected.

Ray hasn't left my side since we got here, but it wasn't until this morning that I find out that he is really down here for a physician's convention. It's bad enough that I am forced here as it is, and I have to actually act like I want to be here, but I didn't think he would be all up under me like that. At first I was pissed, but when I realized that it gave me a free minute to use the phone without having to sneak into another room, I was suddenly elated.

"Why the fuck are you calling me now? It's been three days, and you stood me up. Midori, I can do without the extra bullshit."

"But you won't even let me explain—"

"Let you explain what? That you're so into yourself, you

don't give a damn about me? After all the shit we been through, and this is how it turns out for me?"

Jaydah's going off, but what can I do? Everything she said was true, but she knew I was married going in. When did things change? I knew when she gave me the ring I was in too deep, but my selfish ass stayed. Now look at us. If I were smart, I would've given the ring back and ended it then. Now I'm stuck.

"Jaydah, I understand all that you are saying, but I didn't know that Ray and I—"

"Listen. This is what I want you to do. I want you and Ray to go ahead—"

"Hold on, let me talk," I try to cut her off because I know where this conversation is going, but I'm not really ready for it to end.

"No, you listen. I'm tired, Midori. I'm tired of playing second string to your wack-ass husband, and I'm done with having to wait until it's convenient for you. I can't do this anymore, it's over."

"But, Jaydah, let me—"

"It's over."

She hung up. No goodbye or maybe we can talk later or anything. She just . . . hung up.

I start to dial her right back, but I know there is no use. I figure a few days will allow her some cooling-off time, so I'll just talk to her when I get back.

It's a good thing I did hang up, because a few seconds later Ray walks in. I know the meeting couldn't have been over that fast, so he had to have forgotten something.

"Honey, did I just hear you arguing with someone?" Ray

asks as he rummages through some files he had on a desk in the living room of our suite.

As I figured, he left something he needed at the convention.

"No, I was talking to someone at the office about a patient."

"We're supposed to be enjoying ourselves. Why are you worrying yourself with work?"

The look I give him shuts him down for all of ten seconds. He had the audacity to say I shouldn't be checking my office when we are down here doing business for his. Some nerve.

"You tricked me into coming here so you could work," I say, venom dripping from my voice. I swear he makes me sick.

"Listen, let's not argue. The convention will be over in about another two hours. I have a spa treatment set up for us. Let's just enjoy the rest of the vacation."

He walks over and kisses me on my forehead before leaving the room, and it takes everything in me not to throw an elbow at his rib cage. I hate sneaky shit, and he's always up to something.

When I get up to take a quick shower, I notice Ray's wallet lying on the floor by the table in the living room. Initially I pick it up and set it on the table, but something won't let me walk away without looking inside it. Now, I know I would flip if Ray had gone through my personal belongings, and my conscience is telling me to just put it down and walk away, which I try several times.

By the fifth time I find myself sitting on the bed, going through his wallet to see what he has going on. I find real basic stuff like his black card, identifications, charge cards to his favorite stores, and a few dollars folded up. Flipping through the picture department I smile at photos of him and me on vacations we had taken previously. I can't help but smile at the memories.

As I go further down the fold-out, my warm smile turns into an ugly shriek as I lay eyes on a nude picture of Barbara, the head nurse in Ray's department.

I take the picture out, so I can study it closer. I can't believe the audacity of some people. Here this old wrinkled bitch is stretched out with her legs cocked wide open, smiling into the damn camera. When I flip the picture over, I am even further stunned. Under a sweet little message she wrote on the back of the picture, it is dated for December 18, 2006—Ray's birthday.

Thinking back, I remember all I had to go through to make that day special for him. Jaydah and I had gotten into an argument because she wanted me to go to Norfolk with her to some book signings she had at the Military Circle Mall and other local bookstores over the weekend. Her biggest concern was having to take the six-hour drive by herself, but when she informed me that her publicist and someone she was cool with from her book club and another author agreed to go, I felt a lot better.

She couldn't understand that it was my husband's birthday, and as his wife I didn't have a choice in the matter. His birthday was that Monday, and I couldn't see spending an entire weekend out of town then having to rush back to set things up for him.

Long story short, she left for Norfolk, but not before

giving me a key to her spot and requesting that I be there when she got back. That weekend I went all out shopping for candles and sexy lingerie, as well as setting up a meal plan for dinner that night.

I left for work that morning like I usually did, so as not to draw attention to my surprise later that evening. Ray agreed to be home by eight for a dinner date that I told him I set up for his birthday at his favorite restaurant in Center City. I left the house long enough for him to leave before I doubled back to set everything up.

Ray's favorite color was burnt orange, so I pulled out all of the new linen and window treatments I purchased from Bed, Bath & Beyond, and worked on creating a romantic atmosphere with candles to match. I purchased a bag of peach petals to float on top of the bath water I would run later, and after setting up my dinner menu, I went up and got ready for him, slipping into lingerie that matched the bedroom.

I had a trail of rose petals and candlelight leading from the front door to the bedroom. When he walked into the house, there was a shot of Hennessy on the table at the door with instructions for him to drink it before he came upstairs. I chose Hennessy because I knew after drinking that I was guaranteed an all-nighter . . . hopefully.

Everything was perfect. I had the serving tray set up in the bedroom, all of the candles were lit, and I was smelling and looking delicious as I lay stretched across the bed. I made sure to give our housekeeper the night off, just in case we got into something kinky and it got loud up in there.

The house was completely dark, except for the light from the candles that led a trail to the room. I heard Ray pull up to the house at five of eight, so I stretched out on the bed in a sexy pose for him.

Within a couple of seconds he was upstairs flicking on the lights and pulling clothes out of the closet. My entire mood was cut dead short, and it was like he didn't even see me lying there. I turned off the radio as I got out of the bed because I didn't even want the smooth sounds of Luther Vandross to be mixed in with the words I was about to spit out.

"Ray, is this how you come in? What's all this about?" I asked, trying to stop him from pulling more clothes out of the closet in the process.

"Babe, I'm so sorry. I have to be in L.A. in the morning, and I have a redeye flight scheduled for midnight," he said, finally stopping to look at me.

"But it's your birthday, and I did all of this for you," I said as I turned in a circle pointing to all of the things in the room and myself.

"I know, and I'm sorry. Just put the food and stuff in the fridge. I'll be home on Wednesday night. You can reheat it and we can eat then—"

"You can't reheat lobster, you idiot! I can't believe this!"

"Jaydah, I didn't know I—"

"Fuck you, Ray! Just go on about your business."

He was saying some shit, but I didn't hear anything that came out of his mouth. I was dressed in no time, leaving him in the house. He called my cell phone the entire time, but I didn't bother to answer.

Jaydah had gotten back in town that same morning, and even though I knew she was upset, I went over there anyway.

Pulling up to her condo about forty-five minutes later, I haphazardly parked my car and ran up the steps to her front door. When I walked in, she was busy typing away on her laptop, looking like she had a good groove going. I instantly felt bad about disturbing her because I knew it was hard for her to sometimes even write a sentence.

I set my bag down on the coffee table and reached into the pocket of my trench coat to silence my ringing cell phone. Seeing that Ray was calling from his cell phone meant he had already left the house, so I didn't even bother to answer. I just turned the phone off.

"What are you doing here? I thought you were celebrating your husband's birthday." Jaydah said to me, not bothering to look up from her task. She had a habit of doing that, and she knew I hated that shit.

"Ray had to work," I said, walking toward her spot on the living room floor. I stepped out of my house shoes at the door so I wouldn't track snow on her carpet, suddenly embarrassed that all I had on was the lingerie I brought for Ray.

"Oh, so you came here because your man dissed you, huh? Ain't that something?"

"No, it's not like that. Just like I spent your birthday with you, I had to do it for him. It's only fair."

"Yeah, I hear that. Well, make yourself comfortable and drop that outfit in the incinerator. You bought that shit to wear for him, not for me."

How could I have been so stupid? I know Ray is stepping out on me because he isn't pressuring me for sex at home, and he doesn't care that I stay nights out. I wonder if that bitch has ever been at my house? He specifically told me he had to leave for business, and he was laid up with this bitch?

I can't believe it. I fold the pictures back up into his wallet, taking that one and putting it inside my purse. I will be confronting her as soon as we get back to Philly. I can't believe this shit. I could have been chilling with Jaydah, and here I am stuck on a damn island with this lying-ass nigga.

I tried calling Jaydah back, but she wasn't taking my calls. At this point I am just fed up with everyone. I called the airline to see if I can leave today, but the earliest flight out is Friday afternoon. I'm cool with that. All I have to do is bide my time until then.

I get dressed in a basic terry cloth jumper so I can run downstairs to the front desk. The attendant is nice enough to let me make a copy of the picture after I tell him I am a doctor and need some files copied for a client. I have a few of Ray's papers to make it look official, but I really only copy the picture.

Like he promised, two hours later Ray is back in the room. He walks in on me watching a movie from the pay-per-view listing. I act like everything is normal, allowing him to kiss me on my forehead. He goes into the bathroom to shower and change because he wants us to have lunch with a few people from his office.

Since I hadn't gone anywhere, I just changed into a cute pair of peach capris with a white halter-top and sandals to match. I pull my hair up into a ponytail since it is hot as hell outside, and when he is ready to go, we meet everyone in the dining room in the hotel.

Imagine my surprise when I see Barbara sitting at the table with her husband, laughing as if he'd just told the funniest joke of all time.

It takes everything in me not to drop-kick her ass up out that chair. She gives me the phoniest smile when we approach the table, and I don't even bother to return it. This bitch is sleeping with my husband, and I want her to know that I know. When the time is right, she will know. Two more days and I will be up out of this joint, and with the only person who truly cares about me.

A Sucker for Love

Jaydah

By Friday, Nevaeh is working my damn nerves. I couldn't blame her because she loves hard, but she doesn't give a sister any breathing room. When I told her that we should take it one day at a time, I thought she got it, but when I tried to leave New Jersey without her, that caused a glitch in the matrix that could only be fixed by letting her come home with me. I told her she would have to leave by Thursday night, but here it is Friday morning and her ass is still here.

Another thing that kind of got on my nerves was her being naked all the damn time. I don't know if that's a model thing or what, and I understand that she has a beautiful body, but I don't need to see it 24/7. Damn, let me miss it first. This bitch just insists on having her pussy out and in my damn face whether I want it there or not.

The *Essence* photo shoot went extremely well, and the photo is slated to be on the cover of the June issue. I thought Nevaeh was going to wild out at the photo shoot on some diva shit, but surprisingly she just sat in a direc-tor's chair in the corner and flipped through previous is-sues of *Essence* while we took pictures and went through wardrobe changes.

I was ready to jet then, but I stayed with her Tuesday night to shut her up. By Wednesday, I knew I had to go home because I didn't bring my laptop, and I had to get cracking on the script I was working on, so I wouldn't have to hear Nathan's mouth, come August. *Rich Chicks* is going to be my next best-seller. I can feel it. I just hope that peo-ple feel me on it, since it is so different from *She Belongs to Me* and *Second Time Around.* People just can't get enough of Melissa, but I have some new characters I hope the readers will love just the same.

When I wake up Wednesday morning I breathe a brief sigh of relief because Nevaeh is at the gym. That allows me the opportunity to stretch out on the bed, since she slept right under me during the night. When I get up to get a drink from the kitchen I see the note she left for me on the refrigerator, letting me know she would be back by ten. It is 8:45 AM at the moment.

Deciding to take that opportunity to get some more sleep, I dive back into the bed, only to be disturbed by my cell phone ringing. I start to ignore it, but if it was Nevaeh, she would rush back there thinking I jetted on her. Grab-bing the phone I see that it is Midori, and I start to hit the reject button on her ass, but a part of me still wants to curse her out. I answer the phone with major attitude, and instead of telling her how I feel, I just end it all. I ain't any-body's second choice.

For like four seconds I feel bad, but I deserve better. I give her all of me just to be treated like a second-class citizen. Damn the jokes. I just wasn't in the mood to be strung along anymore. We all know that when you're fooling with a married person they NEVER leave their spouse, so there would be no difference with us.

After hanging up on her, I turn over and prepare to go back to sleep. I really couldn't sleep outside the house anyway, so I hadn't had a restful sleep since I'd been out there.

Finally getting comfortable, I am able to close my eyes, just to be disturbed again by Nevaeh busting through the damn door a half hour early. Giving up any hope of rest, I get up to hop in the shower. I have to get out of here.

While in the shower I am thinking about all the shit I have to get done. Three days was way too long for me to have not done anything.

When I get out of the shower I smell breakfast cooking, but I would be taking it out the door. Hurrying to dry off and get dressed, I could hear Nevaeh fussing around in the kitchen. She would put up a fight, but I had to go. It is just that simple.

"Nevaeh, I'm about to be out. Can you wrap my breakfast up in some foil? I'll eat it on the road," I call from the room while I unwrap my shoulder-length tresses from the beehive it had been in since the day before. I already had what little stuff I brought there packed away, and I double-checked to make sure I didn't leave any panties or personal items. Not that I thought Nevaeh was anything like my character Melissa, but you just never know about people.

"I already set you a plate at the table. Why can't we eat before we go?" she says, suddenly standing in the doorway with a sad look on her face.

I wasn't falling for that shit this time. I had things to do.

"We? I need to get back on the road to beat that rush-hour traffic. I should've brought my laptop, but I didn't and I have mad work to get done," I respond, looking at her through the mirror. We go through this shit every time. I already know she would be crying in a few seconds.

"Okay, well, give me a second to grab a few items and we can go."

"What? Hold on, Nevaeh. We didn't discuss you coming home with me."

I run behind her in the bathroom to talk some sense into her. Couldn't she sense I have an attitude, and I need some alone time? I knew this shit was going to happen, and I should've stayed at the hotel *Essence* was providing for me. Between her being clingy and Midori not doing enough, I am ready to scream my damn self.

"Nevaeh, you can't go. I told you I have things to do. You know I can't concentrate with you on my heels. Didn't we already talk about this?"

She doesn't miss a beat, continuing to throw stuff haphazardly in an overnight bag. I can't believe this chick. It's like what we talked about didn't even matter. I finally had to go up to her and grab her so she would stop. Something is telling me to get out while I could, but I couldn't tell her face to face.

"Nevaeh, you can't go." I spoke to her like I was talking to a child. This was the irritating shit I was talking about.

"Why not? I won't bother you while you're working," she said with a pout on her pretty face she knew I couldn't resist.

"Just come on." I looked at her after a second. Something was telling me to let it be, but I didn't listen. Something I'd later regret.

That was two days ago. I was hoping she would leave yesterday, but she gave me some bullshit about not wanting to ride back home so late at night in a cab by herself. Since when was that an issue? It's been times when she left here two and three in the morning when it's pitch damn black outside to get home, so that bullshit she's trying to feed me is not going to pop off.

I get up early this morning and pack her bags while she is sleeping, and set them shits by the door. I leave out an outfit and clean underwear, as well as a few toiletries so we could expedite this. Waking her up at eight on the nose, I rush her through her shower and breakfast like I really have somewhere to be.

She is mad because I really wasn't going to take her home, but if she was smart she would've driven that nice new Ford Edge she had parked in her garage, but she is too scared I'm going to jet on her ass on the turnpike to think about it. I don't care how she gets home; I just want her ass out.

By nine I shower and eat breakfast, and am finally able to sit back and clear my mind. I still need fifty thousand words in an eighty-thousand word script, and I only have five months to get it done. That's not a lot of time, and I know I have to get cracking if I am going to have this script turned in on time.

An hour later, I still haven't written anything, and I decide to get a snack out of the kitchen. On my way past the door I hear a knock, and I instantly get pissed because I think Nevaeh turned back around. I open the door, prepared to break shit off with her, but I get the shock of my life instead.

"What are you doing here?" I ask, holding my chest where my heart is, not believing my eyes.

"I had to talk to you. I think we need to sit down face to face."

I open the door to let Midori in, still surprised to see her standing there. I didn't expect to see her here since we got into that altercation the other day, but a part of me is glad she came. Walking behind her and seeing her thong at the top of her jeans makes me wet instantly, but I hold it down. I could watch her ass jiggle at any time; right now we had some serious talking to do.

Escape Route

Midori

Yup, I straight left his ass right in Belize. When he left out of the hotel room Friday morning, I got up out of there with the quickness, having a cab take me from the hotel to the airport. Before I left, I took the photocopy of the picture I found in Ray's wallet and left it on the coffee table on top of all of his other papers, so he had no choice but to see it. At first I started to write him a nasty little letter, but I decided against it, instead letting him know that I would be moved out by the time he got home. I put my song by Heather Headley, "The Letter," on repeat so he could listen to the lyrics. I was tired of his cheating ass, and if it weren't for him cheating, I wouldn't have turned to Jaydah in the first place.

I had to take a connecting flight from Jacksonville, Florida, and by the time I got to the Philadelphia International Airport and turned my cell phone back on, I had twelve messages from Ray wanting to talk. I didn't even bother to call; I just caught a quick cab to my house. And once I transferred my belongings from the cab to my car, I went straight to Jaydah's house to set things straight.

I know she said she wanted to end it, but a part of me just won't let it be just that. I hesitated before knocking on her door because when I pulled up to her condo, I saw the woman who was with us at dinner leaving out to get into a cab. I didn't really know what her and Jaydah's relationship entailed, and I didn't want any confrontation.

I wait for about fifteen minutes to ensure she wouldn't double back, and also to get my nerve up. Finally getting out of the car, I go ahead and knock on the door, instead of using the spare key she gave me a while back. That is another thing I have to do. Slow down and stop being so presumptuous. After all, I am still married.

She answers the door with an attitude. Her first instinct was to probably shut the door in my face, but she doesn't. She also doesn't invite me in, which was different for her too.

"Can I come in so we can talk?" I ask her after a few minutes of awkward silence. She is really pissed, and I don't think sweet-talking her is going to work this time.

"We can talk right here," she says, making the space between her and the door tighter by closing the door some.

Damn, she is really mad. "Jaydah, don't be like that. Why can't we talk inside? Besides all that, I'm tired. I came straight off the plane to here. Can I at least have a seat?"

She stands in the doorway contemplating whether she wants to let me in or not.

My face says it all, and I really want to tell her my side of the story.

Taking a step back, she allows me in, but instead of going to her bedroom, she sits on the arm of the couch.

I can't even be mad about it; at least I'm not still in the hallway.

"Okay, so talk. What bullshit did you come to feed me today? And please make it quick because I have things to do," Jaydah says to me, looking as if she can't even stand the sight of me.

Something is telling me even the truth isn't going to be enough, but what do I have to lose?

"Jaydah, I just got back from Belize. Ray took me on a surprise vacation for my birthday, and I didn't know we were leaving until we finished dinner," I say with tears in my eyes, but it doesn't look like she believes me.

"It's funny how all of a sudden you don't know whether your husband is coming or going, when only a few months ago you knew his every move. What's changed since then?"

"So now it's my fault?" I say, flipping the script and hoping that it works. "I am not psychic. How in hell am I supposed to know what that man is thinking? Hell, he's doing shit he's never done before, so what am I supposed to do?"

"You know what, Midori? You got too many excuses, and I just don't have time to try and sort them all out for you."

"So, what are you saying?" I ask, my heart picking up speed. I didn't know what to expect from Jaydah, but I know once she's had enough, she starts to think irrationally.

"I'm saying that it's time for you to go. Get the hell out

of my condo, and don't come back until you know what you want."

"Are you serious?" I ask. She has to be joking, but she gets up and walks toward the door. She hesitates for a brief second then opens it wide, looking at me with hate in her eyes.

"How could you do this to me?" I ask, not believing the outcome of this visit.

"Do this to you?" she says with a wicked laugh. "Honey, you did this to yourself, but it was good while it lasted, right?"

"But, Jaydah—"

"Midori, you got to go."

What can I do? As she wishes, I get up to leave. On the way out I try to look into her eyes, but she turns her head the other way. I never thought it would come to this, even though in my heart I knew it had to. I had a husband, *had* being the operative word, and I knew I would have to deal with him too. I have some serious decisions to make, because I'm not sure if I want to even be bothered.

Once I get out into the parking lot and to my car, I find a handwritten note from Nevaeh on my windshield warning me to stay away from Jaydah. That won't be hard because Jaydah doesn't want me around anyway.

My cell phone is ringing off the hook, and when I see that it is Ray calling, I hit the reject button, then afterward turn the phone completely off. I figure I have enough time to get me a couple of outfits from the house and put the luggage I have in my car now in the bedroom.

I decide on the way back to my house to get a hotel room for a few days until I calm the hell down. I don't feel like dealing with Ray right away, and I still have to get this

Jaydah situation intact. I call my assistant and tell her I'll be taking an extra week off, pretending like I'm just having a dandy damn time out with my husband.

Checking into an Extended Stay hotel by the airport, I dip back out once more to get some groceries to put into the cabinets while I'm there, and after taking a long bath I wrap up in the covers on the bed and drift off to sleep, wondering when my life got so complicated. Extended Stay isn't really my hotel of choice, but I just need to be somewhere quickly, and where I know Ray wouldn't look for me.

The sad thing is, if I had to choose between the two, I'd choose Jaydah because she gives me peace of mind. Ray, on the other hand, offers financial stability, so I have to decide which I can do without. A part of me knows I need both.

Am I Worth It?

Jaydah

I have to get over her. Damn, I hate feeling like this. I swore, after Nevaeh, I would never get involved with another woman. Not only did I do that, but this one is married. The hard part is I really care about her. I mean, it's been over two years. She's been with me since my first novel, and we've been through so much. Not that it's all been peaches and cream, because we have definitely been through shit, especially when it comes to Ray, but at the end of the day is it worth my sanity?

I miss her already, and I know I won't be able to just let her go, but I have to start somewhere. I try to act like I'm not hooked, but it's two o'clock in the damn morning and I'm laying here in the dark, trying not to pick up my phone and call her. Okay, I'll admit that I did call her crib once, but her housekeeper answered the phone and told me she wasn't there.

Against my better judgment, I call her cell phone, hoping she won't answer. Maybe then I'll be able to move past these emotions and go to sleep. I start to just hang up, but then she'll call back and I really don't know what to say. The phone rings four times. Just when I am going to hang up, I hear her voice on the other end of the phone line, and I know at that moment it is too late.

"Jaydah, I knew you would call."

At first I am speechless. I had to hear her voice, but a part of me doesn't want to. What am I supposed to say? *"I know you're married, but I have needs too?"* How selfish is that? I don't have any business fooling around with her anyway, so what does that make me? Yet, I can't walk away. I can't . . .

"We need to talk," I speak into the phone, my voice not sounding like my own to my ears.

"I know, and I'm sorry for everything."

"What happened with us, Midori? I mean, I knew it wouldn't last a lifetime, but does it have to be over this soon?" I find myself close to tears and I hate myself for that.

"Life happened, and it got out of control for both of us. Why can't we go back to how things used to be?"

"Because we're different people now. I can't keep playing second. Where does it leave me?"

We both get quiet, deep in our own thoughts, afraid to really say anything. I go back to how it used to be back in the day when we would hop a plane without hesitation and be laid up on somebody's island somewhere doing whatever. I remember those times when we would go to my book signings and she would pass out bookmarks for me, bringing people over to my table to get an auto-graphed copy of the latest Jaydah B. novel.

I would also go to seminars with her, and I would be so

proud as I smiled brightly in the back of the room, saying her speech with her line for line because we'd practiced so much, I'd memorized it in the process. Before all the lies and bullshit came into play.

"Jaydah, you know I love you, and I would never hurt you purposely," Midori says, practically in a whisper.

My head won't let me say it back, although my heart feels the exact same way. "I know you do, but what do we do now?"

"We start over," she says between sniffles. "We start fresh, and take it from there. That's all we can do."

"And what do we do about Ray?" I ask, curious to see if she is sincere or not.

"He is my husband, Jaydah. I took vows and everything. What can I—"

"Let's just work on us. We'll figure that out later."

We both get quiet again. There are so many things I want to ask her. Like, why did she lie to me about her birthday, for one? Who does that? As a teenager I may have lied about my age, but never the day I was born. That was a good one that I'd have to use in a book one day.

"I called your house earlier. Your housekeeper said you weren't there."

"I'm not. I got a hotel room by the airport."

"For what? Why didn't you go home?" Midori is wilding out. I didn't think it was that serious.

"I don't feel like dealing with Ray right now. I just up and left Belize and came home. He didn't even know I was leaving. I found a nude picture of his office manager in his wallet that was taken on his birthday last year, so I left him the picture with a note on the desk and rolled out. I came straight to you from the airport."

I am speechless once again, which isn't normal for me. I knew Ray was a dog and stepped out, but on the flip side of that, she's been stepping out with me for years. I guess the determining factor would be who dipped out first, but at which point does it matter?

"Which hotel are you at?" I ask, turning on the bedroom light so I can find something to slip into right quick.

"Extended Stay off of—"

"I know where it is. What's your room number? I'm on my way."

After getting her information, I hop into my whip and make it to the hotel in record time. What I like about Extended Stay is that each room has a separate door, unlike most chain hotels where you have to enter into a lobby. The rooms actually resemble moderate-sized efficiency apartments equipped with a small kitchen and necessities that you need for an "extended stay."

Midori answers the door in a sexy red thong with matching bra similar to the one I have on. We share a long hug once the door is closed, and at that moment I know I have to keep her around.

Backing her curvy body up to the bed, we collapse in a heated embrace, neither of us wanting to be the first to let go. With skilled fingers, I unsnap her bra and release her firm breasts into my hands, caressing them appreciatively. Rolling her hardened nipples between my thumb and forefinger produces a long moan between kisses that could go on forever.

Taking the liberty of standing her up and exploring her body, I run my hand across her smooth stomach, everything feeling strange, yet oddly familiar at the same time. Using my fingertips, I expertly reach under the fabric of her thong to find her cut low, the way I like it. When I spread her lips with my thumb and forefinger, her clit practically jumps up at me, producing a quick smile from my own lips at getting reacquainted with a familiar friend.

Removing my lips from hers, I begin kissing down the front of her body, purposely ignoring her breasts because I know she hates when I do that. Instead of allowing my lips to touch her nipples, I breathe warm air on them, causing them to stand at attention. I kiss around the perimeter, then trail wet kisses down her torso.

Instead of removing her thong, I pull it to the side and open her up with my free hand. She smells like peaches and tastes just as sweet, and I lap at her stickiness until she can barely stand.

On wobbly legs, she backs away from me until she reaches the bed, pulling me down on her as she lays back. I fit comfortably in the curves of her body, as if we were made to fit together, and my body feels like I'm on fire.

Her kisses slow me way down, and we enjoy the feel of each other as we intertwine our bodies around each other. Tonight it will just be us. No toys, no music, no rush . . . just the sound of us breathing and the feel of our softness on each other. Our true skills will come into play, and I'm excited about it.

Midori pushes me onto my back and takes my breasts into her hands. My walls are contracting nonstop, and I break out in a sweat from the anticipation of feeling her lips on me.

This was what I needed, but a part of me knows it has to come to an end. Am I being greedy? On second thought, so what if I am? Shit, I have time invested, and she wasn't happy at home. That is all it boils down to.

She plants soft kisses down my stomach, and I spread my legs so she can make it do what it do. Midori comes off all shy and all that, but make no mistake about it, she knows exactly what she is doing. We just had this energy that set the room on fire every time we got together, and I just couldn't get enough of it.

She circles my belly button with her tongue and warms the inside of my thighs with her hands before she takes her place between them.

My breath comes in short pants, and I am almost hyperventilating because I know what is about to happen next. She moves her face closer to my lips and I can feel her breath on my clit when she exhales. I use one hand to hold her hair back from her face, and my free hand to spread my lips so she won't have a problem fully accessing me.

Damn, I can feel her getting closer, and when it feels like her lips are finally going to make contact, her phone starts blasting "My Boo" by Usher and Alicia Keys. I don't have to look at the phone to know who it is. The entire mood changes, and I feel like maybe I shouldn't be there.

She doesn't bother to answer the phone; instead, she crawls up beside me and pulls me into her arms. "Jaydah, I need you. I know it's difficult right now, but I just need some time to figure things out."

I don't bother to respond. I just lay my head close to hers and hold her as tightly as she holds me. I'm not sure if my whole heart is in it, though. My gut is telling me I need to run for the hills.

"Take all the time you need. I'll be here," I respond as I close my eyes.

I have to get back in my grind, and I know being away from Midori is hard, but getting rid of Nevaeh will be even harder. I don't feel like being bothered right now, and it's time to start making some people a part of the change. The question is: Who will it be? Nevaeh or Midori?

Let's Stay Together

Midori

Iwas back home Sunday night—the same night I would have been coming home from Belize with my husband, had I not discovered his secret. Not that it was really that deep of a secret, because I knew Ray was messing around. But when you have solid evidence right in your face, it speaks volumes. That shit hurt, and even though I didn't have room to call a kettle black, I still had feelings.

The housekeeper took the liberty of unpacking my suitcases when I'd dropped them off days ago, and I am sitting on the bed, deciding if I am going to pack another bag for a few more days at the hotel or if I am just going to go ahead and face my husband and get it over with.

So many thoughts flow through my head. I'm trying to figure out if indeed we are really together for love, or is it just for convenience? Do our hearts beat on the same rhythm, or are we merely two strangers passing? Do I love my husband? Does he love me? Are we in love with each other? This is too much going on at one time, and I really don't want to deal with it right now.

I don't feel like dealing with Jaydah either. Am I making things bad on her as well?

Fed up, I decide to go back to the hotel, since I hadn't bothered to check out anyway, just in case things didn't work out at home and I needed to go back. I call my assistant at the office to let her know I will be in the office on Tuesday. I need to take one more day off to get my living situation together.

I know what I have to do, but I can't get up to do it. I'm tired of everything, and my heart won't allow me to get up and pack a bag. I remember lying back on the bed, but somehow I end up falling asleep. It isn't until I hear the front door open that I know I fucked up.

Instead of jumping up, I curl up in the bed and pretend like I am still asleep. I am suddenly glad that I hadn't started packing a bag because then I would have to explain myself and I don't feel like it.

When Ray gets up to the room, I can sense him standing in the doorway, staring at me, but I refuse to budge. I don't want to be the first one to speak because him being here pisses me off all over again. How could he cheat on me with that old bitch? At least, let it have been some real competition.

The weight of his body sitting on the bed makes me open my eyes and look at him. I'm sure my eyes are bloodshot from me just waking up, but the scowl on my face says everything. I'm heated, and in keeping it real, I don't really want to talk about it.

He, on the other hand, looks remorseful, but I don't

trust it. He decided to spend his birthday with his mistress. That is not acceptable. I lied to my mistress so I could stay true to him, and he forgot the rules. How fair is that?

"Midori, I've been calling you all weekend. Why did you leave like that? Why didn't you answer my calls? I left you a ton of messages."

Ray speaks to me in an almost accusing tone that I'm not in the mood for. How the hell does he think he has the audacity to question me and he was the one caught cheating?

"Answer your call for what? So you can tell me more lies?" I come back in an even tone that lets him know I am not going for that shit.

He has a lot of damn nerve, trying to pop fly. He had a picture of a naked woman that I knew in his wallet. It's not like she was some random chick. I could identify her and had seen her on too many occasions. I was forced to break bread with her, and she always gave me a fake-ass smile, like she knew she had one up on me, and in reality she always did. I can't handle it, and honestly don't want anything to do with this sick triangle we are caught in. The only reason she was able to keep her job all of these years was because she is screwing my husband. And her husband and mine were best friends. What kind of shit is that?

"Look, Midori, I don't want to argue with you."

"Then don't!"

He looks defeated when I get out of the bed and go into the connecting bathroom to wash my face.

I should have stayed where the hell I was at because I really wasn't ready to deal with this just yet. It's too fresh. I can still see her naked body, and a part of me hated on her a little bit. Not that I wasn't on top of my game, but for her to look as old as she did, her body is gorgeous. At the same time, when you have a plastic surgeon as a husband, you can look as young as you feel whenever you're ready.

"Midori, can we please talk like rational adults? Let me at least explain myself," Ray pleads from the bathroom door as I scrub my face with Neutrogena facial cleanser.

I guess he takes my silence for an okay, and I decide to let him talk while I floss and brush my teeth. At least if I feel forced to talk, I wouldn't be able to with a mouth full of toothpaste.

He gave me the watered-down version of the love affair he had with Barbara that started a few years ago. Apparently her husband is a whore, and she decided to return the favor. At the time I was just building my practice, and along the way I met Jaydah and wasn't really home much. When I decided I needed to spend more time with him, he was already feeling pushed away and was occupying his time with his mistress, so he didn't want to spend time with me. In the midst of it all, we were running circles around each other and running away from the thing that we wanted the most.

"Midori, I want to make it work. I want a family, and I want to be with you. Maybe we can start from the beginning," Ray says to me in a tear-filled voice that has me choked up on the inside, but I refuse to show how I really feel until I get some things straightened out with him.

"Do you think it's that easy, Ray? Do you think you can just come in here and offer me a thought-out apology that you've probably been practicing on the way home, and everything would go back to normal?" I ask him after I finished gargling. Men, I swear, I hate them, always trying to flip shit like they don't do any wrong.

"My apology wasn't thought-out, Midori," he says in a frustrated voice, like he can't believe I am acting the way I am.

Oh well. You get what you put out there.

"Ray, you've been fucking your head nurse, you have the picture in your wallet to prove it, and you want me to forgive you? Does that sound logical to you?"

"Not when you put it that way, but that was a long time ago."

"It was on your birthday, just a few months ago. I would've never done that to you."

I brush past him on my way out of the bathroom and decide to prepare myself for bed, feeling a little guilty because I have been doing just that for the last few years. I have things I need to do tomorrow, since I decided to take the day off, and I hope one of those things won't include having to find an apartment. Of course, Ray is on my ass, so I have to pretend like he isn't in the room.

Turning my back to him and facing the dresser mirror, I pull my shirt and my bra over my head in one swoop, tossing them into the clothes hamper that I keep next to my dresser. I sift through my pajama drawer, quickly finding the multi-colored sleep shirt Ray absolutely hates. I wear it every time we are mad at each other, so he wouldn't try to touch me during the night. Bending over, I pull off my pants, forgetting that I had on a thong underneath.

Catching Ray's reflection through the mirror, I turn my head the other way to avoid his gaze as I select a lotion from the dresser to moisturize my skin before putting my nightclothes on. I can still feel him watching me as I run my hands across my skin. I snatch my nightshirt off the dresser and slip into it, taking time to put everything on my dresser back in its place.

When I chance a glance back in the mirror, Ray was standing behind me, trying to make eye contact. I don't respond. We just watch each other in the mirror, until he breaks the silence between us.

I am almost certain that my ugly sleepwear would serve as protection for me, but Ray doesn't seem fazed by it at all. Instead he presses his body up against mine and wraps his arms around me from behind in a loving embrace that shocks me at first.

I turn my face away because I'm not ready to forgive him. I'm not ready to feel what I'm feeling, because since the first time I found out he was stepping out on me, I've been determined to never feel that pain again. I blocked it out. I removed him from my heart, and I let Jaydah in . . . or so I thought. Now, I'm not so sure.

"Midori, look at me, please," he says to me, gently turning my face toward the mirror.

I don't know where the tears come from, but it's like a waterfall is in my head spilling from my eyes and dripping from my eyelashes. I don't want to forgive him, but . . .

"Ray, I can't do this anymore."

He is silent, tears streaking his face, causing the sadness in his eyes to look identical to mine. I'm not sure if his tears are because he can't have Barbara anymore and he is stuck with me, or if he feels like he is truly in danger of losing me. My heart won't let me ask.

"I need you. I need us to work. Please, can you give us a

chance? I know what I did was wrong, I know. Please, just let me explain."

I turn from the mirror to look him dead in his face, and I know instantly I am making a mistake. This is the kind of shit people do in the movies when they know they should leave, but they don't, and you find yourself hollering at the screen saying how stupid they are. I am that stupid woman at this moment, but I did take vows for better or for worse. I guess this is one of those "worse" times.

"Okay, let's talk. Tell me everything."

I know I'm putting my life on the line and that I have a way out and didn't take it. I know that if this were a movie everyone would be calling me stupid right now, but I don't care. It's about my happiness, and I am happy with my husband, aren't I? Jaydah was just a quick fix, right?

As we snuggle up in the bed, I lie in his arms and listen to the story he fabricates. I don't believe any of it, but my heart won't let me say a word. Fake it till you make it. Those are the words to live by. I'm just not sure how long I'll be able to.

No Happy Holidays

Jaydah

"Fireworks on the Fourth of July. Thanksgiving was another lie," I sing along with Mary J. Blige, feeling every lyric on this song. She is singing about me and Midori, but I know it's time I move on.

Nevaeh is here using up all my damn hot water. Who the hell takes a two-hour shower? I had to check on her to make sure her ass hadn't dropped dead or some shit, because you know those model types never fuckin' eat. She just showed the hell up, and I was pissed because I hadn't heard from Midori since she went home, and I knew that meant that she and Ray had reconciled.

A part of me wants to hate her because she found the one thing I never could: true love. But when you think of true love, do you incorporate the possibility of a cheating-ass husband and lonely nights? Do you include the tears, and the headaches, and the tight feeling in your chest when you feel like you're going to take your last breath and you don't, but it still hurts? The ups and downs were getting to be too much, but now I feel like I'm in revenge mode, and I don't think I want them happy together. The thing is, how am I going to break them apart?

"Sorry I took so long in the shower," Nevaeh apologizes as she walks past me stark naked and plops her dripping wet ass on my bed.

I roll my eyes up in my head and head toward the kitchen to get something to drink. I want her to leave, but why can't I just say that shit?

"It's cool. I guess I could always take a shower next week," I say in a sarcastic tone as I sit down in front of my laptop. I have a deadline that is creeping right up on my ass, but I can't write. My mind is occupied with so much other shit that I can't even concentrate on the story I'm writing. I know my next book is going to be a for-sure best-seller—that is, once I get the damn thing done.

"Oh, I guess you're on some PMS shit this afternoon, huh?" Nevaeh comes back while she dries off.

A closer look reveals her ass resting on my pillow, and I am so close to snapping, it isn't even funny.

"No, but do you think a shower is supposed to last that long? You only weigh like a buck twenty soaking wet, so what took so long? Then you come walking your naked ass out here, dripping all over my damn floor, and plopping your naked ass on my pillow. I'm confused as to why you don't see my agitation."

Reading over the last page I wrote, I begin typing the scene out that was playing in my head to at least get this chapter done. I have been on this same chapter for two weeks, and I really have to get moving.

I want to call Midori, or just be a fly on the wall in their house so I can see what was going on. I have to move past it, though. At least until I am done with this book.

"Damn, you act like you don't even want me here," Nevaeh says like she is about to cry. But I'm in I-don't-care mode, and it doesn't faze me in the least. "Nevaeh, you invited yourself here. I was just nice enough to let you stay."

"You are such a mean bitch! We are in a relationship, Jaydah, and you act like I don't even exist."

"First of all"—I jump up from the table and take three giant steps across the room to where she is. I have to set the record straight if it kills me—"We are not in a relationship. I told you that I wasn't ready for all that, but you keep insisting on making me be with you."

"And what's so wrong with me that I can't get a commitment from you?"

"Do you think you're perfect? Do you not believe that you can be annoying as hell?" I want to punch her in the damn throat, and I am saying mean shit to her just to hurt her. In reality, she is more reliable than Midori could ever be, but I don't love her. That's all it boils down to.

"And you just got all your shit together, huh? You annoy me too with your sometimey-acting ass, but I accept you for who you are. I don't try to change you."

"I'm in love with somebody else."

It's like time slows down, and everything is in slow motion. Suddenly the sounds around us get louder, and I can hear the faucet dripping in the bathroom because Nevaeh didn't turn it all the way off when she got out of the shower.

I don't want to be the first to break eye contact, but I can't look away. I can hear a car passing by with its speakers to the max, sending out snatches of "One More Chance" by The Notorious B.I.G. into the atmosphere, and at that moment I need just that, another chance.

"What did you just say to me?" Nevaeh asks, like she didn't hear what I said the first time.

Truth be told, I can't bring myself to say it again, but I have to, so I can hear it with my own ears.

"I'm in love with somebody else," I repeat the words, but don't know if I really believed them. Midori has her own situation, and we all knew the side jawn never wins, so what am I in love with? The possibility of her being miserable with me? Because in reality she should have stayed with her husband? Who am I fooling?

"What's her address?" Nevaeh asks me as she begins to blow-dry her hair and press it out with my ceramic flat iron.

She isn't all the way together, and I am wondering what is clicking in her head. I don't want to have to choose between the two because, if I have to pick, I wouldn't pick Nevaeh.

"What do you need her address for?" I ask out of curiosity, knowing I would never give it to her. What is she going to do? Go over there and make a fool of herself when I don't belong to her anyway?

"I just want to talk to her," she replies nonchalantly as she gets dressed in a cute pair of Citizens of Humanity jeans with a matching sweater and a sexy pair of Manolo Blahnik kitten heel boots.

I turn my attention from her and continue working on my manuscript, not paying her ass any mind. Nevaeh is anything but thug, and I know Midori could get good and ghetto, so if Nevaeh knows what is best for her she will fall back.

"Do you hear me talking to you?" Nevaeh asks me again.

I think I'm successfully ignoring her, but apparently I'm not.

"Nevaeh, I'm not giving you Midori's address."

"So what do I do in the meantime? Sit back and play with my pussy until you decide who you want to be with?"

"No, by all means do you, because I most certainly will. I can't concentrate with all of these distractions, and I just need some time to think. You don't have to wait for me."

She doesn't even bother to respond; she simply turns on her heels and gets her pocketbook.

I watch her as I continue to type, and she takes the time to pack up the few things she has here, and surprisingly I don't care.

I need a moment of solitude, and I don't feel like the drama that comes with being in a relationship, as if my being lesbian sometimes isn't enough. It's hard for me to walk out here and do these interviews and book signings and pretend like I don't like the advances so many women make at me, when I know a few of them I would have definitely bedded. I am fed up and tired of everything.

"So you just gonna leave?" I ask her once she has everything packed and is heading toward the door. I hate to see her go, but I know I'd be a fool to ask her to stay.

Her nose is red, and her cheeks are stained with tears as she buttons her coat and wraps her scarf around her neck to protect herself from the harsh March winds blowing around outside. I feel bad. Really, I do, because I don't want it to end like this, but I know it has to. It's time to make Nevaeh a part of the change. I need to sort my emotions out, and I can't do it while she's here.

"What do you want me to do, Jaydah? Huh? What do you want me to do?"

"Forgive me."

She doesn't bother to respond; instead, she pulls her rollaway suitcase through the door and looks at me one last time before closing it.

I thought I was going to fall to pieces, but a part of me in a weird sort of way feels relief. I can't give her what she wants right now, not at this point, and in reality I can't give Midori what she wants either.

Closing my laptop after saving my script, I turn out all the lights after lighting a few strategically placed candles I have around my place. When I go to the bathroom to run some bath water, I am annoyed that Nevaeh didn't even bother to rinse the damn tub out, but in that same instant I know that is one of the things I would miss about her.

Once I rinse the tub clean, I sit inside and allow the tub to fill up while I am in it, making the water extra hot. I know the hot water will soothe the aching muscles in my legs and arms, but there isn't water hot enough in the world to soothe the muscle that hurts in me the most: my heart. I rest my head on my bath pillow and my feet on the faucet, allowing the bubbles in the tub to cover me up to my neck. My life is in shambles, and a part of me figures I deserve as much.

I hear my phone ring, but figure it may be Nevaeh calling to reason with me, and I don't feel like hearing it right now. At the same time it could be Midori, but I don't feel like hearing her shit either. Instead, I allow Mary J. Blige to serenade me because I feel like she felt in the song I have on repeat. For the other woman there are no happy holidays. That statement couldn't be truer, but am I willing to give up all the other days in between?

Sinking further into the tub, I think about going all the way under and staying there until my soul is taken away, but there is no glory in the life of a dead author. The news of my demise would fly through MySpace and all who thought they knew me would speculate, but on the very next day the world would be back to sweating the next best-seller, and I would be a has-been.

After sitting in the tub until the water turned cold and my skin puckered like a prune, I quickly wash in the cool water and make my way to my bed, plopping down soaking wet in the very same spot Nevaeh had occupied. I don't even bother to dry off; I just curl up under the covers and sing along with my girl Mary, while I try to put a plan together. Tomorrow is going to have to be better because, on the real, I am running out of options.

Hypothetically

Midori

"So are you going to do it, or should I?" I ask Ray as we share space at the breakfast table. He is reading the daily news and seemingly enjoying his meal, while I sip a cup of hazelnut coffee, not really tasting it, but drinking it anyway. Ever since I found that picture and the reality of what we were doing to each other set in, I've looked at him differently.

Of course he fed me a bunch of bullshit last night about always loving me and never wanting to leave me. He was so apologetic, but not enough for me to surrender and give him some pussy. Cheating is one thing, but knowing who he cheated with is different. That bitch had been in my house and had broken bread at my table, all with a snide-ass smile on her face. I could just imagine that same ridiculous-ass smile down at the unemployment line. I don't care where she works, she had better have her ass gone today, and I'll be definitely making a surprise visit to his office to make sure it was done. Hell, her husband has a practice; she could go and work for him.

"Should you do what, honey?" he asks me, not even looking up from his paper.

I have to control my reflexes from tossing my hot cup of coffee on his ass, but I play it cool. You can't game a gamer, and if nothing else, I'll have shit my way.

"Fire Barbara. Should I go do it, or will you?"

I'm not in the mood for beating around the bush this morning. Hell, I don't even know why he is keeping her ass around anyway. All she does is sit around the office and talk shit with the other R.N.'s who work there. What is she doing that anyone else around there couldn't do? Okay, she is in charge of distributing meds, but I'm almost certain there is someone there dying to take her spot. No one is liked by everyone.

"Midori, I told you I would handle it. Do I come over and try to run your business? Huh? When I told you that Tiffany was stealing medication from your office and trying to sell it on the street, did you let her go right away?"

"This is hardly the same thing, Ray," I shout at him, having to put my favorite coffee mug down before I use it to bust him in the damn head. "Tiffany was a thief and was dealt with accordingly. Barbara, on the other hand, is sleeping with my husband and causing problems in our household. There is no need for further investigation because the damn evidence is in your wallet!"

"You know what, Midori? You're right. When I get to the office, she'll be called into a meeting."

"If you don't do it, I will. I'll be hitting her husband up

to let him know what's going on, too. Don't fuck with me, Ray. I promise you won't win."

"Are you threatening me?" he asks, abruptly sliding his chair back from the table and standing up to tower over me.

"No, I'm not threatening you at all," I say as I stand up as well. I only come to about his shoulder, but I don't care. The bigger they are, the harder they fall. I don't even bother to raise my voice, but I know what I have to say would hit like a ton of bricks.

"Well, it sounded like a damn threat to me," he says, circling the table and standing right in front of me.

Lord, just don't let me have to go get my little friend from the bedroom closet. I'd kill his ass, then turn around and do the damn autopsy.

"I'm not threatening you, Ray, but I promise you that if the bitch isn't gone by lunchtime, you won't like how shit goes down. It's cheaper to keep me, Ray. Believe me when I tell you, it's cheaper to keep me."

I don't even bother to wait for a response. I simply turn to rinse my cup and set it inside the dishwasher. I can feel his stare burning a hole into the back of my head, but Ray isn't stupid. I have five brothers who are just waiting for him to fuck up, so they'll have a reason to chop him up into little pieces and feed him to the family dog.

Just to be a smart ass, I take the keys to my car, and to his on the low, so he will have to move out all the other vehicles he has in our five-car garage to get to the jeep he drives when he isn't driving his Phantom to the office. Normally he would have already switched spaces with the

Phantom, and when I see that he hadn't swapped cars yet, I take advantage of the situation.

We park in the driveway because, who feels like having to back out of the garage every day when, if the car was right there, we could get in and bounce? I don't care either way. Since he wants to make shit hard on me, I'll be making it hard on him.

After my drive in to my office, I park my car in front of my building, and after checking to make sure everything is running, I walk two blocks down, battling the wind to go to the Starbucks coffee shop, so I can get some scones and another cup of coffee, since I'd neglected to eat breakfast. The wind is whipping up some kind of crazy, and I have to almost walk backwards to keep from being blown away.

As I attempt to do just that, I bump into a soft body, and instantly regret it. I don't want to turn around because I think it may be Jaydah stalking me, but to my surprise it is Nevaeh. I haven't been in the same space with her since dinner that night, and I'm kind of surprised that she knows my name.

"Midori, how are you?" she asks me with a bright smile that suddenly makes it feel a little warmer outside.

I am stunned by how beautiful she is, and I can't take my eyes from her face. "I'm good. How have you been?" I finally respond, stepping into the warm embrace she offered. I can smell her Pink by Victoria perfume wafting up from under her scarf as we embrace, and I close my eyes and inhale for a quick second, trying to remember and forget at the same time how it feels to be held by a woman.

"I'm good. Just had to drop off some shots to a photographer not too far from here."

"And how is Jaydah?" I ask on the sly, just to see if she

will answer the way I want her to. I want her to say she is going through it and she doesn't know why, so I can tell her it's because of me, but she doesn't say that. In fact, her answer takes me totally by surprise.

"Oh, girl, I can't keep her off me. Mmmm, she just got me turned the hell out."

"Is that so?" I say in response, not sure how Jaydah would feel about her just outright telling people her business. Not that Jaydah is shy with the fact that every so often she wants a soft body in her bed, but she doesn't just go around saying that shit to total strangers either.

"Honey, I'm pressed for time, but check this out. What are you doing for lunch today? I want to talk to you about something," Nevaeh says, seemingly oblivious to the fact that she just told me she's gay. At the same time she piques my curiosity, and makes me wonder what she has to talk to me about.

I was actually planning to go over to Ray's office to set a few of them bitches straight and to make sure he gets rid of Barbara's bitch ass, but what Nevaeh has to say seems a tad more interesting. It's cool, though. I'll just make it a quick lunch with her so I can still jet over to Ray's office and have time to get back for my afternoon patients.

"I should be free around that time. What did you have in mind?"

"Let's meet at the Lotus on Chestnut Street, let's say, around one. We could have a nice light lunch and chat. We have a lot of catching up to do."

We exchange numbers, and I hurry back to the office to get my morning started.

I zip through patient after patient, letting my staff know to transfer a few of my patients to the other resident doctor so I can take a late lunch. By twelve I am done, out the door, and sitting at the Lotus fifteen minutes early, waiting for Nevaeh to show up. At first I thought this was a setup, but when I see her walking into the restaurant ten minutes later, I know I made the right choice by showing up.

"Hey, Midori," she says as we embrace, and her perfume made its home in my nostrils again.

If I was the type, I would definitely bed her ass, just to get back at Jaydah, but for me it isn't that serious. I just want to know what she wants to talk about.

We place our orders for salads and hot tea, which are served to us immediately. We both take several sips from our tea and a few bites from our salad before we begin to speak.

"So, what did you want to talk to me about?" I ask as I bite down on a crouton and lick the dressing from my fork.

Her eyes follow the sensual movement of my tongue, and I pretend like I don't notice, as I tease her with what she could possibly have.

"Jaydah was telling me that you and Ray were going through it, but she wouldn't say exactly why. Was it about her?"

I am surprised at just how bluntly she posed her question, as if she was simply asking me about the weather or where I got my shoes. I decide to tread lightly because this feels like a setup, and if I know Jaydah at all, I know she wouldn't have spoken about us to any woman. Nevaeh was jealous, and she came here to puff her chest out and let me know that she possibly has won. Little does she know that if indeed she does get Jaydah, it would be because I handed her over, not because she took her from me.

"No. Why would you ask that?"

"I was just wondering. Jaydah is so fidgety around you, and if past experience serves me correctly, that means she has a thing for you."

"Well, I'm flattered that you think so, but Jaydah and I are just acquaintances. There's nothing there that I could think of, and besides all that, I'm married," I say, flashing my ring, which set Ray back a several thousand dollars.

"I know enough to know that a ring doesn't mean shit, but I totally understand. Please excuse me, though. I was simply inquiring."

"Hey, there's no love lost, especially since I didn't know you and Jaydah were an item, but do tell her I said hello."

"I certainly will. As a matter of fact I'm on my way there now. My pussy has been throbbing all day, and we both know she's good at fixing little problems like that."

I don't even bother to respond; I just simply enjoy the rest of my salad, while my silence seems to eat at Nevaeh's nerves. I know she wants me to wild out and act a fool, but you got to wake up a little earlier in the morning to get me pumped.

As she gathers her belongings and gets herself together to walk out, I wish her a wonderful day and blow her a kiss, causing her cheeks to turn beet red.

"Hey, don't forget to tell Jaydah I said hello. Better yet, have her call me."

That was the highlight of my day as she turned and stormed out of the restaurant, almost tripping out the door. I swear, I crack myself up.

Finishing the rest of my tea, I take my time to get myself together and mentally prepared for what could possibly go down at Ray's office. I'd hate to have to resort to my old ways when I was a young girl from the bottom of West Philly ready to knock a bitch dead in her face. I'd like to think that I am grown and sexy and could handle a situation better than that, but if I walk into that office and Barbara is still there, there's going to be trouble—trouble, said in my best Dollar Bill voice, à la Bernie Mac from *The Player's Club.*

I pay the bill, leaving the waitress a hefty tip because I like the shape of her lips. I think to get her number, but know that it is this kind of behavior that got me in trouble in the first place. Once settled in my Vanquish S, I ease into traffic and head uptown. Hopefully I won't have to act a fool, but we will soon see.

Consequences and Repercussions

Jaydah

I hear glass smash and the car alarm go off and die down after a few minutes, but for whatever reason, I don't move. In fact, I roll back over and fluff my pillow before dozing back to sleep. I haven't heard from Nevaeh in a couple days, and Midori for over a week, so I don't think that whatever drama is going on outside has anything to do with me. My dream picks right back up from where it left off, and it is starting to get good too. But my gut keeps telling me to get up and look out the window.

My condo is on ice, despite the cold weather outside, but that's the way I like it. I'd rather throw on some night-clothes and pull out an extra blanket to keep warm before opting to turn up the heat. Dragging myself from under the covers and out into the freezing cold, I decide that since I am up I might as well use the bathroom, since I had been holding my bladder for the past four hours because I was too lazy to get up.

As it is freezing cold in there, I handle my business as quickly as possible, so I can wash my hands and look out the window. My gut starts getting tight, and I just know something is wrong. I just hope it isn't my shit.

I go over to the window and pull the shades back, temporarily blinded by the sunlight streaming in. Jogging my memory to remember where I had parked a few days ago, my mouth drops open when I make eye contact with my car. A tear involuntarily slips from my eye as I look at what used to be a hot whip parked in the same spot as my car.

"I'm losing my mind. I must have parked somewhere else." I talk out loud to myself as I rush into my bedroom to look for a pair of shoes to put on. I don't want to believe that my car is fucked up like that, and I have to go take a closer look just to be sure. I try to be rational at first, hoping that maybe I had parked closer to the building where my car was out of view, and that the car I saw belonged to someone else in the building.

I rush outside, and to my disappointment I didn't parked my car next to the building like I wanted to believe, but I'm not ready to believe that's my car sitting there looking a mess. Even when I get up on it, my mind won't accept it. I walk around the car, checking out the slashed tires and scratched paint that reads BITCH on the door and hood. The brick that sits in the window caused the glass to spider out and crumble where it lies.

This is some bullshit, I say to myself as I run my finger across the black permanent marker that graces my back window. It is a drawing of a stick-figure woman in tears and a huge broken heart next to that, but I still don't want to believe this is my car. When I get to the back of my car, what I've tried to deny for the past few minutes rings true. Sure enough, that's my license plate staring back at me.

I keep my cool, surprisingly, and take the walk back to my condo like I have it all together. I pull out my insurance information so I can make a claim and call the police, so I can have a report before I do so.

As I sit and wait for them to arrive, I toss the thought back and forth in my head on whose ass I am going to put my foot in. Let me retract that, I already know that I'll be heading up to South Jersey to visit Nevaeh, because Midori definitely has more class than this.

By the time the cops get here I am already dressed, have eaten, and am watching an old episode of *Martin* on TV One, getting my laugh on. I still can't believe how calm I am, but I know I won't be able to maintain my cool for long.

The cops badger me like I wrecked my own car, which makes me want to fuck Nevaeh up even more. I give them all of the information they need, and once they are done, I call the insurance company to report my claim. By the time they get done playing "a thousand questions," I am mentally exhausted.

They set it up so I can have a rental car, and Enterprise was nice enough to come and get me, so I can fill out my paperwork and drive off the same day.

When I leave there, I head home to pick up a few things and then point the car toward the New Jersey Turnpike and make my way to Nevaeh's house with a bat in the backseat, and my mind set to beat her ass. I flip through my CD's for some riding music, but all that comes to mind is Biggie's *Ready to Die*, but on the flip, I am ready to kill.

About an hour and some change later I pull in front of

her house, disappointed that this simple bitch was bold enough to park her car in the driveway. I would have had my shit hidden if I had done some crazy shit like what she did, but it's cool. I'm here to teach her a lesson.

Now, my first instinct is to wreck her shit like she wrecked mine, but I have bigger fish to fry. Taking the key she gave me from my back pocket, I let myself in after grabbing the metal bat from the backseat of my rental car. Her place is unusually quiet, and I think maybe she skipped town on me and shit.

I am prepared to wreck her place, but when I hear a noise come from her bedroom, I creep my way over there to listen more closely. I can hear Dr. Phil on the television telling someone how they needed to get their shit to-gether, and I laugh. Nevaeh will need more than the good doctor's advice by the time I'm finished with her.

I grab hold of the doorknob, deciding to make a quick entrance and catch her off guard. Let's just say, the look on her face is priceless when she sees me standing in the doorway. This simple heifer has the nerve to be dressed in lingerie, like she is expecting me to come and shit. Too bad I have to beat her ass for what she did.

"Hey, I wasn't expecting you," Nevaeh says, looking at me then back at the television.

I can't believe she's going to act like she doesn't know why I'm here. I don't even respond. I just lunge at her from the door and commence to beat the shit out of her. I take every frustration that I've had with her and whoever else and use that energy to beat the life out of her. I have her by her hair, so I can get a good swing at her face, and I am suddenly glad that I dropped the bat in the living room before I came in because, otherwise, I'd be locked up for a murder one rap.

She doesn't even have a chance. She tries to swing back, but the blows are going so fast that she doesn't know whether to run, or stay and try to fight back. I must have banged her head up against her headboard a million times, and not in a loving way like when I'm over here twisting her back all crazy. I don't know how much time has elapsed, but by the time I get done, there is a bloody mess on the bed and Nevaeh is crying uncontrollably.

"Now, the next time you decide you want to fuck up my car know who you're fucking with. Forget you even know me."

I don't even bother to look back; I simply toss her key over my shoulder and scoop up the bat from the floor so as not to leave evidence. When I leave I feel a lot better, but I feel horrible at the same time. I'm not even the abusive type, but what she did was unacceptable.

During the drive home I feel like shit, and almost call her a few times, but decide against it. She deserved that ass-whipping, and I'll do it again if provoked. You don't just take it upon yourself to mess up someone's property. I think about reporting her ass, but care a little too much to fuck up her career. I know I am done with her for sure, though. I won't even miss the pussy, because she's a damn nag and I am tired of her anyway.

I drive past Midori and Ray's spot before I go home, using my binoculars to see if I can peep them from the road, but when I don't see anyone's car in the driveway I pull off, thinking that maybe she is a waste of time as well. "I just need to be single," I say to myself as I drive. Honestly, when I don't have anyone occupying my time, I get a lot more accomplished.

I pull up to my house a little while later, noticing that my car is still sitting there. I almost shed a tear as I take a tour around the damage one more time. If the bitch is going to slash my tires, she should have slashed all of them. Who the fuck only slashes three tires, like I could drive off on one? I remember that I didn't bother to get my key back from her, and she has keys to my house and my whip. I'm changing the locks on the crib anyway just because, but I doubt after the beating that I gave her that she'll show up around here again. Besides, I'll be getting another fat royalty check in a few weeks, so once I get my car back, I'll be right at the dealership, trading it in for something better.

Walking back to the rental to grab my bag, I walk up to my place. I immediately strip and run some hot water in my Jacuzzi tub. I soak in a nice hot bath to relax my sore muscles. My shoulder is extremely sore—I guess from all the swinging I did—and my knuckles hurt from punching her ass all hard. The more I think about it, the more I regret it and the more I want to call, but you don't do that kind of shit to someone then call back to apologize.

I think about Midori and what I'm missing with her. It's been a while since I've had my body pressed about against someone soft, and my hands lead a trail that I know Midori's tongue would have easily followed. I slip two fingers into my softness and use my other hand to caress my nipples as I try to bring myself to an orgasm. I think I may have to call her and see what's up.

Just as I was getting into it, a loud, persistent knock

echoes through my condo from the front door, and it pisses me off instantly.

"Who is it?" I yell from the bathroom in frustration, knowing I wouldn't be able to hear them if they answer back. Damn I'm pissed, and it shows as I climb out of the tub and track water around my apartment because I can't find my bathrobe. I finally see it hanging on a chair in my bedroom and rush over to put it on.

"Who is it?" I yell again as I get closer to the door.

Whoever it was, was knocking like they were going to take the damn door off the hinges.

"It's the police," a masculine voice came from the other side.

I wonder briefly what they are doing here, then think maybe they are coming to get more information on who wrecked my car. I don't see the need to bring up Nevaeh's name because I already dealt with her, so I'll just tell them I don't know who did it.

"Yes?" I say with a slight attitude once I open the door. The wind rushing in makes my bare nipples rock-hard and strained against the soft terry cloth of my bathrobe, and my clit pulsates from the wind touching me there, because I have no hair there to protect it.

"Are you Jaydah B. Wells?" the officer asks, once he finally picks his tongue up off the floor.

"Yes, why do you ask?"

"I am here to place you under arrest for assault and battery on a Nevaeh Thompson. You need to go with us to the police station."

"Assault? Are you serious?" I ask, not believing this bitch had the audacity to call the law on me after what she did to my car.

"I am serious, ma'am. We need you to come down to discuss the situation, but it's only gonna take an hour or so and you'll be out."

"Okay, can I at least put some clothes on? I can't go down there like this."

"Sure, you can put on something, but we have to come inside to ensure you won't try to escape from the window or something."

I don't even bother to respond because I am too upset. How in hell am I going to escape through the window from the tenth floor? I go into the room and grab a thong and a pair of socks, and walk down the hallway. I stand right in front of the officers half-naked while I dress in the clothes I had on earlier. Both of them try not to look directly at me. I grab my purse off the couch and put on my coat, preparing to walk out with them.

"Ma'am, it's procedure that we have to cuff you, but we will do so after you secure the premises, and I will put them on in the front so that it's more comfortable for you."

I can't believe what I am hearing, but I comply, so I could get this shit over as soon as possible. The ride over is only about ten minutes, and once they place me in the cell, I know my stay will be going downhill from here. Nevaeh is going to pay for this shit, and she's going to wish I had killed her ass instead.

Ring the Alarm

Midori

I pull up to Ray's job delighted to find a parking space right next to his car. That way, if one of his workers says he isn't there, I'll know they're lying. I am in battle mode, and I just hope he did the right thing. I'd hate to have to wild out up in this camp. I check my lips to make sure they are nice and glossy and that my hair looks good before I get out and go inside.

The waiting room is packed with patients waiting to get to the back to see the doctor. I am surprised, because Ray's office normally runs pretty smoothly, so the current chaos is more than likely the result of getting rid of Barbara. The two medical assistants at the front look like they are just about at their wits end, having to deal with all of these disgruntled patients by themselves. I hear one of the workers tell a patient that she has to reschedule because they are so far behind. Frankly, it is all hilarious to me, but that's what you get when you step out on your marriage with a bitch who works with you on the job.

Now, I'm not going to lie to you. That little meeting I had with Nevaeh has my head spinning, but I have more pressing issues to deal with than some jealous ho who is sweating over a chick that I'm not even sure I want. Surprisingly I haven't heard from her in a while, so I guess she finally decided to do what I asked. That's a first.

I don't even bother to ask of my husband's whereabouts, because he had better be in the conference room handling his business. The two medical assistants look at me strange when I walk behind the desk and to the back, but if they value their jobs they will shut the hell up and do what they have to do up front.

It's like everything is a blur as I approach the door. Putting my ear to the door to listen for what's happening before I go inside, I can hear someone crying and two other people talking, so I know they'd gotten around to doing what I said. I don't bother to knock. I walk right in on the meeting and over to where they are.

"This bitch has the audacity to show her face after trying to sabotage me? How dare you come here!" Barbara screams at the top of her lungs, afterward attempting to lunge at me from her seat.

I don't even flinch because I've been itching to beat her ass since forever. Just to let her know I'm not intimidated, I take my time taking off my coat and taking a seat not too far from her. I hope she'll give me a reason to bash her skull in today.

"Midori, what are you doing here? I told you I would handle it," Ray says to me through clenched teeth, like he is ready to strike me as well.

"I came to make sure that you would," I say, looking at both Ray and Barbara, daring them to try and make me leave. I smirk at Barbara because she looks a mess from crying, her makeup running all over her face.

"You never liked me," Barbara screams at me from her seat, breaking down even further.

"Why should I? How long have you been fucking my husband, Barbara? How long have you been smiling in my face and eating at my table like you weren't enjoying my husband in my bedroom when I was gone?"

"I'm not like that," she cries, looking around the room desperately as she tries to make eye contact with Ray and his office manager.

I am the only one who maintains eye contact, enjoying watching her lose her mind. "Oh, you're not like that? Do you really believe what you just said?"

"Fuck you, Midori! You've always been jealous of me and Ray's relationship."

"And rightfully so, since you've used our bed for marital duties more than he and I, but it's cool. Y'all can have each other," I reply, cool as a cucumber as I take my coat from the chair to put it on so I can leave. This is getting to be too much, and I don't feel like the drama anymore.

"I didn't sleep with your husband—how many times do I have to tell you that? He and my husband are friends. Why would I do that?" Barbara cries hysterically, hiccupping and trying to catch her breath.

I'm not moved by her act at all, because we both know what the truth is, and I don't want to have to go there on her, but what choice do I have?

"So, you're going to stand in my face and lie? You're going to stand here and deny the truth, like I'm slow to what's been going on with y'all? Why did you think you were being fired, Barbara?"

"Raymond said it was creating a conflict of interest in the office, and I was voted out by the staff."

I look at Ray to confirm, and when he turns his head the other way, I know what she said was true. He didn't even have the heart to tell her that I knew. I feel bad for a second, but her husband and I were the true victims, and I am going to make it my business to tell him what's up before more lies are spread.

"Barbara, you and Ray deserve each other, and as I mentioned, you can have him. The reason you are being let go is because you are creating a conflict of interest between him and I by having an affair. That's the whole situation in a nutshell."

"I'm not sleeping with your damn husband!" she shouts at me again, and at that point I know I have to take it there.

"Barbara, I hope you get your situation together soon. When you're at the point when you believe your own lies, it's a sickness."

"But I didn't—"

I hold my hand up to stop her mid-sentence because I am just tired of everything. I take the time to zip up my coat and grab my purse from the chair. I start to walk away, but when I feel the photos in my pocket, I know I have to put it out there. Turning back around, I take the pictures and the copies that I made from my pocket and scatter them across the table. I found more pictures of Barbara and Ray, both together and by themselves, in Ray's closet. I can't take it anymore.

Barbara almost passes out, and the office manager has to catch her before she hit the floor.

"Like I said, you've been fucking my husband. Ray, I want a divorce."

I don't even bother to wait for a response. I simply turn and exit the room, closing the door behind me so they can have some privacy. As I walk down the hallway I see everyone looking at me strangely, but I don't care. I have my own heart to deal with, and I have to hold my own on this one.

On my way back to my office, I wrestle with the idea of telling Barbara's husband what transpired between us, but I have to because I had already FedEx-ed him an envelope with the pictures in it to his office, due to arrive tomorrow. I have to tell him, and feel it's only right to give him a heads-up on the situation.

I have two patients who were just sent back and are waiting for me, so I go in to them first before I make it back to my office. I don't want to make the call, but if it was me, wouldn't I have wanted someone to let me know what was going on? I dial the number before I decide against it and resist the urge to hang up the phone before someone has the chance to answer. I was doing the right thing, right?

"Thank you for calling the Corrective Surgery Center of Philadelphia, where looking your best is our number one goal. This is Audrey. How may I direct your call?"

"Hi, Audrey. This is Midori Hunter, Ray Hunter's wife. Is Dr. Evans in?"

"Hello, Mrs. Hunter. Yes, he is, can I place you on hold for a second to see if he's available?"

"Sure, you can."

"Okay, please hold."

Instantly the lyrics to Anita Baker's "Fairy Tales" starts

playing while she has me on hold, and I find myself singing along. My life used to be a fairy tale, but not in a good way. All the lies and deceit . . . it's just too much. I briefly wonder if I should just let it go, but in reality I have to say something. I try to get it in my head what I am going to say to him, but the truth is all I have. No sugarcoating it.

"Mrs. Hunter, I'll be transferring you now."

Before I have a chance to respond, I hear Mike's booming voice on the other end, and he sounds like he is in a good mood. That only means that Barbara hasn't told him what happened at Ray's practice yet, and in a way, that gives me an advantage, because I need to let him know what's really going on before any more lies are told.

"Hey, Midori. How are you today?" he asks in his usually cheerful voice that always makes me smile. That was before today.

"I've had better days." I sigh into the phone, trying to mentally prepare myself for what I'm about to do.

"A hectic day at the office, huh?" He chuckles into the phone, oblivious to the news I'm about to share with him.

"Mike, I need to tell you something, and I hope you forgive me for what I have to say."

"Sure, Midori. Is everything okay with you and Ray? What do you need to talk about?"

I take a deep breath and begin to spill my guts about everything I found out about Ray and Barbara and what they'd been doing behind our backs.

We are on the phone for a good hour, and I spill everything to him. It was only my hearing him breathe on the other line that I know he's still listening. I feel horrible about what I did, but we both deserve better.

"Midori, is all of what you are saying true?" he asks in a choked-up voice, like he's trying to get it together.

"That's everything I witnessed with my own eyes."

"Listen, I hope you're still sitting down, because I have something to tell you as well."

My heart begins to beat faster than it ever has, and I know I'm not prepared for what I'm about to hear. I can hear Mike take a deep breath before he begins to talk, and as life as I know it begins to spiral downward, I know by the end of the day I'll need to be taken to a crazy hospital to be checked in.

Locked Down, Locked Up

Jaydah

That bitch got me locked up. I still can't believe this shit. I've been in this bitch for three days, and am yet to get my first phone call. I absolutely refuse to use the toilet in this cell, and when the C.O. finally figures out that I'm not playing, he walks me down to use a bathroom in an empty cell, where he stands and watches my every move.

"You got ya clit pierced?" he asks me after I wipe myself and stand up to pull up my clothes.

I start to say some smart shit to him, but figure he'll be my only ticket to having a halfway decent time in here without any extra bullshit, until I see the judge in the morning.

"Did you see a clit piercing?" I flirt shamelessly, hoping that maybe it will land me an empty cell where I can think better without having to sleep with one eye open.

"Yeah, I did," he responds, damn near drooling.

The dick isn't usually my thing, but he seems content

with just being able to eat the pussy, so I decide to test him to see how far he'll go.

"How you see my little ol' piercing from way over there?" I ask after I pull my pants all the way up, just to see if he'll let me leave or if he would stop me from going. My money is on the latter. I know if I let this fool just get a sniff of it, he'll be putty in my hands.

Just as I thought, he walks his simple ass right where I am and backs me into the bench, causing me to sit down unwillingly. For a second I think I had made a mistake because if he tries to rape me, I have no back up. I know I have to get control of the situation, and fast, before shit gets out of hand. I grab him by his tie and pull him to my face roughly, so he can see I am in charge.

"You wanna eat my pussy, don't you?" I say in a seductive whisper.

He nods his head like he's a mute and can't part his lips, never mind the fact that I just took a fresh piss and have been in here three days without touching some soap and water, but I guess maybe he likes it like that.

"Okay, this is what I'm gonna do, but I need you to do this for me."

I make a bargain with his nut ass that I know he'll take. I wonder briefly what requirements it took to be a prison guard because they fall for the most gullible shit. I've heard stories of female guards getting pregnant by inmates, and I didn't really believe it, but this dude just confirmed the obvious. They're an easy lay.

I tell him I'll let him eat me out for ten minutes if he moves me to a cell where I am by myself. If he lets me do that, he could eat me out for another ten if I can use his cell phone to make a call. He agrees, and I tell him to just tell the others that I was feeling sick and was moved to another holding cell.

"What if they get mad?" he asks, almost like he was scared.

I simply put my hand into my pants and dip my finger into my slit. His eyes follow my hand down, and when I pull it out he opens his mouth up, ready to suck my finger dry. *Nasty bastard.*

"Do you care if they get mad?" I ask him.

He shakes his head back and forth because he's too busy sucking my fingertips to answer with his mouth.

"That's what I thought. Slide up so I can take my pants off."

He does what I say, undoing his tie like he's about to really feast. His simple ass. I swear, men are so stupid sometimes.

I lay on the cold concrete floor, hoping a damn bug or some shit won't jump out on my ass. He wastes no time diving between my legs and taking me into his mouth.

For a second I can't believe I have stooped this low. Letting a dude taste for a phone call? Is it really that serious? It doesn't even matter at this point, though, because I already made the deal, and he isn't getting up off me until his twenty minutes are up.

I pretend like he is Midori, as my mind flashes back to that time when we were in New York having a late-night dessert in Central Park. It was summer, maybe ten or eleven at night, and we had just come from seeing a movie. We were enjoying sundaes from Cold Stone Creamery on the park bench while deciding if we were going to take the ride back to Philly or cop a hotel in Jersey on the way down. I had book signings at a couple of stores over there, and we visited one of her friends who had a practice not too far from the park before we went to see the movie, so we just kind of ended up there.

"Do we have a Cold Stone back in Philly? I could think of a couple of things we could do with this Founder's Favorite." Midori seductively licked the side of her ice cream cone.

I knew what her tongue was capable of, and was instantly jealous that I wasn't that ice cream cone at the time. I loved Midori because she was spontaneous, and I knew if I pushed her enough, I could get her to do whatever I wanted right here in this park.

"Why do we have to wait until we get back home? Let's see what we can do with it now," I said to her on the sly, just to see if she would take the bait.

Her eyes lit up mischievously, like she knew where I was going with it, but I could see her tossing it around in her head like she was afraid of getting caught.

"Girl, we not back in Philly. What if we get locked up for indecent exposure? I can't call Ray to get us out, you know."

"We won't get caught. Follow me."

She looked like she was scared to death, but I wasn't. I had on white capris and a cute tangerine pair of Steve Madden peep-toe pumps to match my halter top. I didn't want to get my knees dirty, so I took Midori's sweater from around her waist while we were walking so I could kneel down on it.

She had on the perfect outfit. A sexy little white skirt that came down to just above her knees, with a yellow halter top identical to mine, and a cute pair of yellow-and-white Baby Phat stiletto sandals we'd picked up from the mall on the way to New York.

If I knew Midori as well as I thought I knew her, I knew she didn't have on any panties under her skirt, and that would make it that much easier. I pulled her in between a cluster of bushes that were tall enough to hide us between the trees, and since it was dark out and there were barely any people outside, I knew we would be cool.

I spread her sweater out on the ground, much to her dismay, but once I put my head under her skirt and started to go to work on her clit, she forgot all about her sweater getting dirty. We were right in the middle of the bushes, so she couldn't lean up against the trees, and I could feel her body sway a little as she tried to balance on one foot while her other rested on my shoulder. She was clean-shaven, and it was welcomed. She pulled her skirt up and held it in her hand so she could watch me work, and I was determined to give her a show.

I used one hand to part the lips of her pussy, and using what was left of my cone, I smeared some ice cream across her clit, sucking it off and putting more back on there, until she begged for mercy. I would take some of the ice cream into my mouth and stick my cold tongue into her tunnel, causing her body to shiver in spite of the humid night air.

She cursed me out under her breath, between orgasms, about getting her sweater dirty, but she only wore it in the mall because it was a little chilly. It ain't like it went with her outfit. Besides, it wasn't anything that couldn't be dry-cleaned.

I devoured her right under a full moon, and needless to

say, we barely made it to Jersey. By the time we got to the hotel the clerk was looking at us like we had gotten into a fight, because of our disheveled appearance, but in reality, we were tearing each other apart on the ride over.

Just as I begin to cum, I come back to, taking a glance at my watch. The prison guard's face looks like a glazed donut as I rub my pussy from his eyebrows to his chin trying to build this nut up. We are just coming up on twenty minutes, and he doesn't seem like he is going to stop, so I knew I would have to finagle some shit through this phone call.

Since he is eating me so well, I may have to make two phone calls, but I need to call Nevaeh first. I have to warn her ass that an ass-whipping is due for this shit.

"Don't forget about that phone call you owe me," I politely remind his ass, stopping him briefly from doing what he was doing. He is actually pretty damn good, but I have to handle business.

He doesn't say a word; he simply pulls out his cell phone and passes it to me, diving right back in between my legs.

The first person I call is Nevaeh, but she doesn't answer her phone. I start to leave a nasty message, letting her know I will be coming back for her ass, but I don't want her to use it against me in court, so I hang up.

Since guard guy is still getting his eat on, I take the liberty of calling Midori, but I get her answering machine as well. I guess she and Ray are working it out after all. I try to leave a message, but her mailbox is full. *I can't believe this shit.*

As I close his phone, I look down at him having a damn

field day, and gently pull him from my pussy so I can scoot up. His face is completely glazed over, and the top half of his shirt is soaked with my juices. I almost want to laugh at how dumb he looks, but decide against it, since I may have to use him later.

"That's enough for now," I say to him as I get up from the floor and slide my pants back on, my vagina lips feeling slick against my panties. I take the liberty of punching my number into his cell, at least until I got out of here, just in case I need another favor. He looks disappointed that it was over, but once he sees me putting my number in, he has a smile on his face.

"You can take me back in there with the rest of those bitches. I don't want to hear no shit from any of them."

He doesn't really have much to say, walking around all obvious that we did something, with that big dumb smile on his face. I have to tell him to wipe his face off while we are walking back to the holding cell before we get too close. When he lets me back in there everybody is looking at me strange, but they all know not to question me, because I have attitude written all over my face.

"Come on tomorrow morning," I say to myself, leaning my head against the wall. Hopefully by then I will be able to post bail and be out of this hellhole, and back to handling my damn business.

I wish for a second I had my laptop with me because I could have put some of this bullshit in the book I was writing. At least I would have been able to get some of it done.

Another Relationship

Midori

I'm speechless, not believing a word that comes out of Mike's mouth, but believing it all at the same time. He was in cahoots with all this madness? Everybody knew but me? Am I truly the last man standing? And apparently this shit has been going on for a couple of years now, but how am I just now finding out? Am I so absorbed with Jaydah that I can't see my own home falling to pieces?

My head is spinning, and I can feel a serious headache coming. Just as he was quiet, only breathing, while I talked; now it is my turn to be mute.

What it all boils down to is that the Evans are swingers and had recruited my husband a long time ago. The plan was to bring me into the mix as well, but for whatever reason, it never happened as planned.

Mike informed me that this had been going on since a few years after we met, all of us going to the same med school before branching out into our individual fields. Although he and Ray often shared his wife, he had no idea she was seeing him on her own. That wasn't in the agreement. Initially it was supposed to be a trade-off, his wife for me, and we were all supposed to kick it. But I never liked his wife and dove straight into building my practice, so they just kept it as a threesome.

Mike keeps me on the phone for at least an hour, just as I did him, and we conclude our conversation with my letting him know to expect a package from Federal Express tomorrow with the pictures I had found inside.

I hang up the phone even more confused than before I called. I'm not even sure if I warrant the right to be mad, because in all honesty, we stepped out on each other. Ray just got caught slipping, but who's to say he hadn't caught me and just didn't say anything? I'm hurt and confused and spiraling out of control, but who can I talk to?

I sit staring at the wall, lost in thought, when my cell phone begins to ring out of nowhere. I can't find it at first, and by the time I locate it in the bottom of my junky pocketbook, the phone has stopped ringing. Flipping the phone open, I press the button for my missed calls list, and I don't recognize the number that is listed. Normally I wouldn't even call back, because everyone I talk to is already stored in my phone list, but I push the talk button anyway just to see. Maybe it was Ray calling and he used someone else's phone because he thought I wouldn't answer his call.

The phone rings four or five times before someone answers it, and I don't recognize the voice on the other end. I give my phone a puzzled look, like the person on the other end can see it.

"Yeah, who dis?" The person on the other end answers the phone all ghetto and shit.

I know for sure at that moment this person isn't anyone my husband or I know.

"Umm, someone called my phone not too long ago, and I was calling back."

"Oh, I think li'l shawty called you. Hold on," he says before I can ask who he was exactly.

Who does he know that I know? It isn't long before my curiosity is quenched when I hear Jaydah's voice on the other end of the phone.

"Midori, it's Jaydah. Nevaeh got me locked up," she says into the phone, almost like she is whispering.

I can hear dude in the background telling her to hurry up before she uses all his minutes on his prepaid phone, and I can't believe what's going on.

"Locked up? When?"

"Three days ago."

"Where are they keeping you?" I ask, grabbing a pen really quickly so I can write the information down.

All I hear is Fifty-fifth and Pine, before the phone clicks off. When I call back, an automated voice says that person can't be reached, meaning she must have used all of his minutes.

It is already evening, so I figure I'll just go up there tomorrow afternoon on my lunch break, if she is out by then. I briefly wonder why she hasn't seen the judge yet, since it was a weekday, and what really went down with her and Nevaeh? Seems like sis was causing problems everywhere, and whatever happened with them, she probably deserved it.

Once the office is locked up and I talk to my co-workers out front for a while, I get into my car and drive around for a minute before going home, since I am certainly in no rush to get there. I wonder if Ray knows I talked to Mike and if Barbara knows what I had told him by now.

I wonder what my parents would think of me, and why my marriage hasn't turned out as wonderful as theirs. They celebrated their forty-fifth wedding anniversary this year, and they seem to be still in love. And it's not like I don't love Ray, because I do, but where did we go wrong? Scratch that, I know where we went wrong, but how do we fix it? Is it even worth fixing? Do we even want it fixed?

I pull up to my house an hour later, trying to be optimistic about the situation, but in reality I know it's a wrap. There isn't any trust in our relationship, and in all honesty, how could there be? We're too busy snaking each other. Maybe Ray can explain to me where I went wrong, and vice versa, so we can come to a mutual decision about this. Barbara, I'm sure, is at home trying to make things work with her husband, so I have to see what I could do with mine.

When I walk in I notice that the house is awfully quiet, but I know Ray is home, because I saw his car parked outside. I stop in the kitchen to grab an apple off the counter as a stall tactic, because I honestly am not ready to face him yet. Taking a bite, I figure if my mouth is full, I won't have to talk right away.

Upon entering our bedroom I practically trip over Ray's Louis Vuitton luggage that is stacked up by the door. The room looks like a hurricane swept through it, and I don't see Ray anywhere.

"Ray!" I call into the bedroom, stepping over his luggage and walking toward his open closet door.

He is inside pulling out suits and shoes like he is a mad

man, and although I am standing there, he brushes past me like I am invisible.

"Ray, where are you going? Why are you packing?"

He brushes by me again, this time giving me a nasty look that silences me instantly.

Is this the result of our meeting with Barbara earlier? Is he trying to leave me?

"Don't you hear me talking to you?" I stop him when he comes back to walk by, and he snatches his arm from me, looking like he is ready to put my head through the door.

"Oh, I hear you. I hear you loud and clear, but guess what? I'm done listening."

"What's wrong? I mean, besides the obvious. But why are you leaving?"

He stops in his tracks and looks at me.

For the first time in all of the years we've known each other, I can't tell what he's thinking. Okay, so Ray gets on my nerves, but I'm sure I work his nerves as well. For a long time I wondered why I was with him, but for the first time, I can't see myself without him.

"You know what, Midori, I've tried my hardest to make you happy. I did. All I ever asked you in return was for a family, but I was willing to wait until after you'd built your practice."

"Hold up, this is not about a family or my practice. This is about you stepping out on me with Barbara. I spoke to Mike, Ray. I know what's been going on with y'all."

"I know what's been going on with you too. Seems like I wasn't the only one stepping out on this marriage."

"What? You must have bumped your head on the way home. Who did I get caught with?"

I am pissed beyond recognition. There is some truth in

what he said, but I didn't flaunt my shit like he and Barbara did. What ever happened to discretion? And he has the nerve to stand here in front of me and try to throw it back in my face, like he is the one losing out? I'd rather be here alone than deal with this nonsense.

"You didn't get caught. I'll give you that, because you were smarter than I was about the situation. But guess who isn't the only one who likes to take pictures?"

He is just about working my nerves, talking in riddles, but I'm not really worried because I was extra careful when dealing with Jaydah. We went out of town most of the time, and besides that one time in Central Park, we didn't do the public-display-of-affection thing. She really wasn't the type.

"What are you talking about, Ray? What pictures do you have of me? Just because you did some stupid shit and slept with your co-worker doesn't mean I was out there doing the same thing."

He doesn't respond, and that scares me the most. What does he have on me? We were so careful, and I am confident that he has nothing on me . . . almost.

He goes to the door and ruffles through one of the many bags he'd packed, coming up with a packet of pictures inside of a Kodak envelope. He tosses them at my feet and leans against the dresser, folding his arms across his chest in a menacing manner that has me shook for a second.

I bend down to pick up the envelope, not sure I want to see what's inside. So many thoughts go through my head at once as I see photos of me and Jaydah from as early as last February when we were at the Writing for Success conference in Atlanta. We'd walked through the fair on each other's heels, and the pictures seemed harmless. It just looked like two girls hanging out together. The kiss we stole in the elevator on the other hand, was clearly photographed, and I wonder who could have taken it. We were on the elevator by ourselves, so when did that happen?

I am at a loss for words, and the pictures get more detailed as I flip through. There are some at Jaydah's place and a few at hotels when we were out. I was set up, and I already know who's behind it. I just hope I don't end up sitting next to Jaydah in jail, because it is definitely about to go down.

"Ray, listen. Both of us were wrong, but I think we can work through it. Please, don't leave before we have the chance to talk it out."

"I thought you were done talking," he says with a sneer, as if I am wasting his time.

"Ray, please . . ."

He looks like he is tossing it around in his mind for a while, then he finally sits down on the bed.

I don't know where to start, but I know what I have to do. First, I have to fix this, at least for right now, but I am on a mission and I need to talk to Jaydah to get the information I need.

Rewind My Heart

Jaydah

They have had me sitting around in the holding room of the court for like six hours. There were at least twenty of us waiting to see the judge, and they fit us in between people who had court dates on the same day. The court-appointed lawyer who showed up on my day of questioning informed me that the reason I was in jail for so many days was because Nevaeh actually came down and filed for a protection order, having showed them the cuts that were up and down her arms. Now, I will say this. I whipped her fuckin' ass, but I didn't pull a knife on her. I guarantee you that the simple bitch cut her arms herself and blamed that shit on me.

At the end of the day though, it was her word against mine, and I had no scars or bruises to show for it, except for a few scratch marks on my arms from her trying to defend herself.

Yes, I know that her wrecking my ride wasn't enough reason to beat her the way I did, but there are two things you just don't mess with: my car and my money—unless, of course, you're just trying to get on my bad side on purpose. I was pissed, but regretted it a little. Maybe I should have just stayed home and reported the accident without going over there. The thing is, when you're dealing with women like Nevaeh, they won't just stop coming around. She would keep showing up and doing spiteful shit until I forgave her and let her back in or she finds someone else to stalk. I don't have that kind of time.

I'll also have to explain to Nathan why I have yet to turn in my completed manuscript. Honestly, this chick has me stressed the fuck out and I can't write. Between worrying about suicidal-ass Nevaeh and trying to juggle Midori at the same time, I'm burned out. I guess that's what happens when you burn a candle from both ends.

I see some prisoners being escorted back to the holding area without even getting a chance to see the judge, and I don't know what that's about, but I silently hope they don't do that shit to me. I'm not sure if Midori has shown up because I can't see into the courtroom, although I've tried to sneak a peek every time the heavy metal door was opened. They are not playing around here either, and the officers passing through have to put in a code every time they want to open the door.

By now it's like four in the afternoon and my stomach is growling. All I had was the steak bagel meal my little prison guard friend snuck to me early this morning when he first came on shift, and by now that shit is long gone.

Just when I think I can't sit another minute, my name is called to go before the judge. Apparently, the judge sees all the people who come to court on their own before those who are already locked up. That's why we had to wait so long. I guess they figure, since we've been waiting all this time, what's a few more hours going to hurt?

I step into the courtroom hoping for the best, and I notice immediately that Midori is not here, but Nevaeh is. She isn't looking like she was in a crazy accident, with a neck brace or no shit like that, but I can see the remains of a black eye and scratches on her face. She also has on a three-quarter-sleeve shirt, and I can see some of the cuts on her arm. That bitch is on some real *A Thin Line Between Love and Hate* shit, acting crazy and hurting herself just like the chick in that movie.

The judge is fair, I'll give her that, allowing me to explain myself and the situation that landed me in jail. I want to say that this simple bitch was upset because I didn't want to be with her ass anymore. I want to tell her that she was a nuisance and didn't want to give me space, and in reality I didn't really want to be bothered with her, because I was in love with another man's wife. I wish I could have told her that this dizzy bitch wrecked my fuckin' car, and I went over there and beat the shit out of her, but in all honesty I didn't put a knife to her.

I want to tell her that I could be home finishing my damn manuscript and because of this retarded heifer I was stuck in jail for the last three days, but instead I calmly explain the situation and, although I did knock her out the box, I didn't cut her.

The judge looks at me like her head is spinning and she can't believe the words that have just come out of my mouth.

Nevaeh is trying to get me on some domestic violence shit, but we would have to have first been a couple before

it's considered domestic, so what is she talking about? I
hope she knows that there isn't a snowball's chance in hell
that she and I will have any form of communication once
this is over.

I just can't wait to get home. I just want to sit my ass in
the tub and get back in the swing of things, like before I
started fooling around with her crazy ass. I made Nevaeh a
part of the change before, and she begged to come back,
but this time I am cool on her ass.

"Ms. Thompson, please approach the bench," the judge
says as she glances over her glasses before looking back
down at her paper and scribbling something else on there.

Nevaeh looks all scared and shit, like she was just called
to the electric chair, and she has every right to be.

I swear if my wrists and ankles weren't shackled together and we weren't standing in front of this good judge,
I'd be all over her ass again.

The judge looks at both of us for a long time, like she's
trying to look into our souls. I maintain eye contact so she
can see that what I had to say was true. Nevaeh's simple ass
is staring at me instead of the judge, and I can feel her
burning a hole in the side of my face, but I refuse to even
acknowledge her ass.

"Ms. Thompson, who cut your arms up like that?" the
judge asks Nevaeh, while still keeping her eyes on me.

I keep my eye contact on point and hope like hell she
tells the truth.

Nevaeh is silent, looking from me and back at the floor,
then back to me, like the answer will jump out of my head
and into hers.

I'm willing her to tell the truth, and I try not to shuffle

my feet in impatience. I briefly envision myself wrapping my hands around her throat, but snap out of it when I hear the judge repeat her question.

"Ms. Thompson," she says, leaning forward and commanding Nevaeh to make eye contact. "Who cut your arms up like that? Did Ms. Wells do that to you?"

"No, she didn't," Nevaeh speaks to the judge in a low voice, like she was scared to say something.

I don't release a sigh of relief right away, though, because I can tell her mode of questioning isn't done.

"So you're pretty much saying you're in contempt of court, Ms. Thompson?" the judge asks, leaning back into her seat and continuing to write and take notes.

"She beat me like I was a stranger!" Nevaeh hollered at the judge, afterward breaking down in tears.

"Shit, she wrecked my ride. What was I supposed to do?"

"Did you do those things to Ms. Well's vehicle that she said were done?"

"Yes, I did, Your Honor."

"Do you feel safe?" the judge asks her, making more notes.

"No, Your Honor," Nevaeh responds.

I look at her like she is crazy. I've never in all the time we were kicking it put my hands on her, unless it was to please her. I turn to look at my lawyer, but he motions for me to turn back around. Good thing his ass was free, because if I had paid money, I'd be pissed right now.

"Do you want a restraining order against Ms. Wells?"

Nevaeh doesn't answer right away, and I hope like hell that she says yes so I can ask for one also. That way I'd have a reason to not be near her ass even if she tried to pop up on me. I am done with this shit, for good.

The judge continues to write, and after making us stand

there forever, she finally decides she will let me leave, pending I sign some documents stating that I will stay away from Nevaeh and not try to contact her. My lawyer asks for a restraining order for me as well, the first thing he did right all day.

After about another hour or so, I am unshackled and allowed to make a phone call, be it a cab or someone to come get me. They give me my belongings back in the meantime, and when I am finally allowed to make a call, I call Midori. Hopefully she'll answer her phone.

I see my little guard friend, so I knew if push comes to shove, I'll just use his phone or get him to get me another call. I'd promised him twenty dollars for another five-hundred-minute card after I got situated, and that seemed to make him feel better.

To my surprise, Midori answers on the first ring, and she doesn't hesitate to come and get me, letting me know that she has to talk to me about something as well. She sounds upset, but it doesn't even matter, as long as I am getting out of here.

She pulls up a half hour later, and I hop in the car without hesitation. She doesn't say a word to me, and she certainly doesn't act like she's happy to see me. I figure some shit went down with her and Ray, and we are coming to the end of the road. I'm cool with that because I'm tired of the runaround myself. But I'm no fool. I'll let her say it out of her mouth first.

When we get to my crib, I wait to see if she will say something, but she wants to come up and talk, so I let her. That's cool with me, and I rush up to my condo, eager to take a bath. I fiddle with my keys for a second, but once I'm able to get in, I wish that I hadn't.

My condo is turned upside down. Pictures, crystal, and vases are broken on the floor, shattered glass everywhere. My bed is ripped to shreds, and there is a space missing on the wall where my forty-inch plasma television used to sit. That was a gift from Nevaeh, so I already know she was here.

I'm not concerned about all of that because that's just material shit I can replace. I start looking around frantically, lifting up couch cushions from the floor and hyperventilating.

"Jaydah, what are you looking for?" Midori asks, concern thickening her voice because she probably can't believe what she's seen either.

I can't even answer because I lost my voice five minutes ago when I walked in. The tears that flow from my face start clouding my vision, and I have to sit down. I fall to the floor in a dramatic fashion and crawl to the kitchen, where I spot it sitting on the counter. My laptop.

I rush over to it and am happy for a second because when the cops came I was in the middle of a chapter I was working on and never got the chance to save it. I hope like hell Nevaeh had a heart and didn't do what I think she did.

My kitchen is the only space in my condo that wasn't sabotaged, for whatever reasons, which were beyond me, but at that moment I could care less. I take a deep breath and flip open the top to my laptop, pressing the power button immediately. While I watch it go through the motions of powering on, I hold my breath until I am ready to pass out.

"Lord, please let this be right," I pray to myself in a soft voice. That computer holds my entire manuscript that I was working on, plus the beginnings to several book ideas I had been considering writing next. My entire writing career is on my laptop, and I hadn't saved a lot of it anywhere else yet.

When my programs finally come up and I can finally see what was going on, it is just what I expected. Every file, program, game, and picture I had on my laptop is gone. My laptop looks fresh, like I just got it. When I click on a few things, I realize the bitch had restarted my computer and erased my entire C drive.

I sit down heavily in my chair, not believing my luck. The Internet hadn't been set up, so I can't check and see what I had, but I do have some stuff saved to my Yahoo! account, and I hope I have enough of my book saved that I won't have to start over.

Before I close the top, I do notice a notebook file with my name on it, but I know it's some shit that Nevaeh had written, and at the moment I don't feel like reading it. I am going to get her ass back, but I am going to make sure I don't run into her. She is going to get hers, just like she gave it to me.

Decisions, Excuses

Midori

There is no way in the world I can break up with her now. Not when I am seeing her in this condition. Damn, the girl was locked up for three days and came home to a wrecked condo. Not only that, the one thing she held dear to her heart . . . gone. Like she never even had it in the first place. Nevaeh knew how important this writing thing is to Jaydah. How could she do such a cold-hearted thing? Why would she risk her getting dropped from her publishing company for not having her story turned in on time? Nathan, from what I know of him, is an understanding man, but at the end of the day he has a business to run. I am mad for Jaydah and want to go whip up on Nevaeh myself.

I take careful steps over the stuff strewn on the floor throughout the place until I get to the kitchen because I am still stuck on stupid at the front door from what we walked into. If anything, and I know she probably doesn't want to hear it right now, I have to let her know about the pictures my husband has of us and that it is possible her place is bugged. If Nevaeh were smart, she would have removed any evidence of cameras or recorders out of there, but I doubt if she was smart enough to do so. If anything, she was stuck on revenge and forgot all about it.

"Jaydah, I know now is not the time, but once I tell you this I think I have a plan," I say to her as I take a seat at the table, wondering why this is the only room in the entire place that was not messed up.

"Midori, just spill it. Honestly, it can't be any worse than what I'm already living through right now. As a matter of fact, I'll make it easy for you," she says, hopping up from the chair and walking toward the living room door.

I follow behind her, not sure of what she is about to do. She walks to the door and opens it up. I can see the tears streaming down her face, and for the first time ever, I know Jaydah is really hurting inside. She wasn't really the crying type, not unless it was serious. This time I think she's had enough.

"I know you can't be with me, and instead of dragging it out just go," she says to me through sad eyes, and my heart breaks instantly.

I'm stuck at first, but I can't just leave. Now most people would say how stupid I am and I should just take the opportunity to jet when I can, but am I truly happy with my own situation?

"Jaydah, listen to me." I walk up to her and close the door. I'm close to tears myself, but one of us has to hold it together. "Nevaeh set us up, and I know how we can fix it."

I tell her all about the pictures Ray showed me, and although I wasn't sure how he got them, I'm almost certain that they were sent to his office, since that was just a matter of typing in the hospital info to get the address. She must have had someone follow us though, and for a second I feel like I am on that show *Cheaters,* where they catch people on the low doing shady stuff to their spouses.

I tell her everything, and we agree that it's time to make it official. I will be letting Ray know that I am leaving him today. We need some time apart, and I don't want to stay in that house trying to figure it out. He can stay there until I decide what I really want to do.

I tell her the plan I have to get Nevaeh back as well. We'll go to her house at night when it's dark. Jaydah says she parks her car in a designated parking spot every day, so more than likely it will be there, since Nevaeh's banking on Jaydah following the rules of the restraining order.

"So, this is what we're gonna do . . ."

I talk to her while we take a moment to straighten up the place. Everything that's broken, we throw out, and what we can't fit in the incinerator, we carry out to the dumpsters out back.

It isn't long before we have everything cleaned up. Jaydah's sofa is a pull-out, so she says she's cool with sleeping on that until she's able to go out tomorrow and purchase another pillowtop mattress. Nevaeh was even petty enough to take the television out of her room, so we watch television in the living room.

Jaydah doesn't even want to look in the room she used as a home office, fearing that Nevaeh probably tore shit up in there too, and I try to get her to at least see what was up, but she's losing her mind at the moment and refuses to think logically. Surprisingly, when I open the door, it looks as though nothing was touched. That's a good thing, because Jaydah will be able to retrieve a lot of her stuff from her email account, and even though Nevaeh restarted her laptop, we found out that she was kind enough to store Jaydah's book in her flash drive. That doesn't mean we aren't still going to get her ass back, though.

My plan is so hot, I have to step back and kiss myself.

Once Jaydah is showered and lying down comfortably, I make sure she's okay and I roll out, reminding her to be ready tomorrow afternoon when I came. We need to go to Home Depot to pick up a few things for what we have to do tomorrow night. I've already been gone longer than I needed to be, so I have to get home. I have to at least let Ray think shit is copasetic, until I figure out how I am going to jet on his ass.

I see Jaydah's car looking a mess, and I understand why she wilded out the way she did. You don't mess with no-body's whip.

I jet across town to my house, pulling up behind Ray's car. We had been working overtime for the last couple of days, trying to get me pregnant, and I hope it never worked. The very next day after he was talking that I'm-gonna-leave-if-we-don't-start-a-family shit, I had one of my medical assistants give me a Depo-Provera shot on the low. I didn't feel like that shit right now, and hope he never decides to question me and get extra tests done.

I don't feel like arguing with his ass, and he doesn't have the right to be mad. He's been cheating on me for years. Men kill me with that shit. They can go out and do whatever they want, as many times as they want, with as many people they want, and it's okay. Let my black ass step out there and get caught, and it's like the world is about to end. I hate him.

When I walk in the house, he's in the kitchen eating

grapes and working on his laptop. He doesn't even bother to look up when I come in, and even though I speak, he doesn't bother to speak back. He's been doing that for the last couple of days. That's cool with me because I don't feel like talking anyway. Fuck him. I make myself a sandwich real quick and take my ass on upstairs to prepare myself for tomorrow.

Deciding to take a shower, I lock the bathroom door before proceeding because I made the mistake of not doing that two days ago and he came and fucked me in the shower, making me feel like a rape victim afterward. I felt so violated. Even last night he waited until I was good and half-'sleep before he took it upon himself to pull my panties to the side and shove himself inside of me, afterward rolling over, like nothing happened, and falling asleep. I was tempted to smother his ass during the night, but I didn't feel like going to jail for murder right now.

In the morning I get the same attitude. He comes down and eats the breakfast I cooked him without so much as a good morning, and would roll out without saying a word. I guess he would be mad if he knew that I didn't even bother to at least rinse yesterday's breakfast off the plate, opting to reuse it for his breakfast this morning.

"So you're just not going to speak?" I ask him when he joins me at the table.

He doesn't even acknowledge my question with a mere grunt; he simply takes his seat and begins buttering his toast.

This is why women grind up glass in their husband's food and feed it to them. "Ray, I asked you a question—"

"Midori, honestly, you can save your conversation for someone who gives a damn. I just need to eat breakfast so I can get going."

I want to drop-kick his ass. Who the fuck does he think he's talking to? I don't even honor that shit with a response, because in the end I'll have the last laugh anyway.

Once he's gone, I call Jaydah to make sure we're on for today. It's important for Nevaeh to be home when we go there because my plan is brilliant. I want to get her back probably more than Jaydah. I'm not really worried about Ray because I don't feel like putting him in his place right now, but I'll get with him in a minute, after I fix this shit with Jaydah.

Take What You Give,
Even Your Lies . . .

Jaydah

"**B**ut, baby, are you happy without me?"

Nevaeh actually got up the nerve to call me. I want to curse her ass out, but Midori has yet to tell me her plan, so I figure I'll just be nice to her for now. That way, sneaking up on her will be a lot easier. I entertain her for a while before I grab my house phone to call my cell, so the other line will click.

"Can't say that I'm totally happy, but what made you do what you did to me? Why did you mess my car up like that?"

"I was jealous, baby. I thought you were going to choose that married bitch over me. What do you see in her anyway?"

I have to take a deep breath. I want to say, "What do I see in you?" But I decide to let it be what it is. I'll get her ass back; that's the bottom line. I dial my cell phone number into my house phone so I can get this chick off the phone. I'm about to say something I'll regret later, and I don't know if this is a trick or not, since she's got the restraining order on me.

"Hey, Nevaeh, let me call you back. That's my mom on the other line."

I don't even bother to wait for a response. I just hang up the phone. I still have a little over an hour to meet Midori at the Home Depot in South Philly, so I go ahead and get dressed, so I can be there a little early. To my surprise she's already there waiting on me. She must really want revenge on Nevaeh.

She told me on the phone that her husband was acting crazy, so she walked ahead into the store and I trail behind her while we talked on our cell phones. Grabbing a basket, I fill it with the things she told me to buy, including two tubes of Krazy Glue and a tube of Gorilla Super Glue that is supposed to hold tighter than anything in the world. I buy all the things I need without question, and she follows me to Jersey so we can make it happen. By the time we take the hour and some change drive to Jersey, it's dark outside, just the way we need.

When I pull into the parking area, there are two spots close to the building. I suggest we park there because I know, just like in my building, Nevaeh won't be able to see the cars from her window. I have a rental she wouldn't recognize, but I'm sure she'll remember Midori's car, since she was driving the same car we saw when we met them at the restaurant that night. I don't want to take any chances.

I use the key she gave me a while ago to get into the building and am upstairs in no time. Midori suggests I call Nevaeh to see where she is in the house and to just talk to her while she handles her business. I walk down the hallway some, so she won't hear me on the phone while I watch Midori work.

I'm talking some ol' slick shit to her, getting her panties wet and all that, and at the same time I'm in awe of how shiesty and sneaky Midori is. She starts with the tube of Krazy Glue, and squeezed the entire tube into the locks on the door and the doorknob, using a small fan on her key chain to dry the glue faster. She then takes the Gorilla Glue and lines the entire outside of the door where the frame and the door meet. Once I dig what she's doing, I have to smile at her genius.

Nevaeh won't be coming out until the morning, and the package says the glue is quick-drying, so it'll be completely dry in the morning. It's hilarious because she won't be able to open the door, and she was just telling me that she has to fly out to Paris for a fashion show tomorrow. Guess she'll have to climb out the window, never mind she lives seven stories up from the ground.

As soon as Midori gets done and has all of the evidence bagged up, we make our trip back to Philly, with me leading the way in my car. Midori and I never got the chance to really talk the other day after we saw how Nevaeh messed up my condo, but I know whatever it is has to be said. Once we get back to the city I think she'll keep going to her home, but I see through my rearview that she gets off behind me, and is following me to my house.

I pull up close to my building and wait for her to pull up beside me. When she gets out, she gets in my car and pulls out an envelope. I wait for her to say something because I don't remember sending her anything. She empties the contents of the envelope into my lap and looks straight ahead.

There are pictures, tons of them, of us in all kinds of compromising situations. There are pictures of us in my place and some we took of each other when we were out of town. After a while I start looking at the angles in which the pictures were taken and the view appears to be coming from where my dresser sits. Was my place bugged? I thought maybe Nevaeh was a little crazy, but now I know for certain that her elevator doesn't go all the way to the top.

She had to have dipped in my personal stash as well, because some of the pictures were from Punta Cana when we stayed at the Iberostar Resort. We enjoyed ourselves all over that suite and took exotic pictures of each other that I looked at for weeks once we got home. Hell, a lot of the photos were the key point of my many masturbation sessions. I kept them in a wood box under my bed, and Nevaeh's jealous ass must have found them. I know one of the trips was around Nevaeh's birthday and she was mad because I wouldn't be spending her day with her.

All I can do is flip through the pictures and sigh. What was I thinking, fooling around with her? I want to apologize to Midori, but I can't get my mouth to say anything.

"Those were sent to my husband," she says in a sad tone.

I don't know for sure how to take it. Is she upset because we did what we did, or was it because her husband found out?

"Midori, I didn't send these pictures to him." I try to apologize, not really knowing what to say.

"I know that, but there's a lot going on right now. I

think I need some time to get my head together and figure out my situation. I don't want to lose you as a friend,
but I just don't know what to do right now."

"Hey, take all the time you need. I understand."

We look into each other's eyes for what feels like the
last time. We both have some straightening out to do in
our lives, and we need time to do that.

She takes my hand into hers and squeezes it tight before
getting out and driving off in her own car.

I'm glad we did what we did to Nevaeh, and I smile as I
walk up to my condo and begin to look for any hidden
cameras she may have forgotten to take out.

I don't have any business messing around with Midori
anyway, and if I'm going to have her, I don't want to have
to share her with anyone. Besides all that, I have a book I
need to finish. I guess now I have plenty of time to do it.

Smoke

Midori

When I get home Ray is there and gives me the third degree on why I'm late. He claims that he wanted us to go out with some people from the office, but how does he think I would even consider that, after the embarrassment of what happened with Barbara? I try to ignore him and just go ahead and make dinner, but he is seriously talking out the side of his mouth and is about to catch this frying pan upside his head.

"I need you to come to the office and take a pregnancy test. You should have been pregnant by now."

I stop in the middle of cutting up boneless chicken breast to look him in the face. Is he serious? I want to take the very knife I am cutting with and poke him in the damn heart with it. He's taking things too damn far. Now I was trying to be compromising even though he's been acting like a fool lately, and even though his ass stepped out too. But he has to think I was born yesterday, if he thought I was going through with that shit.

"Ray, have you lost your damn mind? I'm not coming down there to do shit. It'll happen when it's supposed to."

"If you don't come to the office, I'll have someone come here. You decide which one you want it to be."

"You heard what I said. I'm not doing either."

"Why? Are you taking birth control? Or did that dike bitch knock your insides loose so you can't carry any kids?"

For the second time that night I am stunned into silence. He's really testing me, and I have to close my eyes for a second and take a deep breath.

When I look up, he has a stupid little smirk on his face like he won the damn discussion. I will take so much pleasure in bursting his damn bubble. This entire situation is working my nerves. I mean, we've been through shit before and have gotten past it, but this is just lingering on too long for my liking.

"Do you know how stupid you sound right now? And you call yourself a doctor." I laugh out loud more to myself than at him. "That same dike bitch you're talking about, you wanted to lay, remember? You wanted me to talk her into having a threesome after we had dinner at the restaurant, remember? I guess old wrinkled-ass Barbara wasn't enough."

Before I can blink, Ray is in my face, his hands wrapped around my neck, choking the life out of me.

I grip the knife tighter, contemplating stabbing his ass with it, but decide it isn't worth it, instead opting to punch him as hard as I can. He lets me go long enough for me to plant my knee in his groin and run around to the other side of the counter.

"Midori, I'm sorry," he pleads with me, trying to catch his breath.

I'm seeing red, and I know I have to get out of this kitchen before I do something I would regret.

"Stay the fuck away from me!"

I turn and run upstairs locking myself in the room. Throwing myself on the bed, I cry and cry, not believing this shit is happening to me. I should have just stayed at Jaydah's house, but I was confused about that situation too, and that would have just made this situation worse. I want to call her, but my cell phone is in my pocketbook downstairs, and I can't remember her number at the moment. Besides, what would I say to her? "My husband is beating my ass and trying to get me pregnant to keep me away from you?" I move to the middle of the bed and curl up in a fetal position, trying to rock myself to sleep.

A while later I can hear Ray testing the doorknob to get in the room, and I sit up completely in the bed. The only thing in the room I have to defend myself with is Ray's gun, and I'm not trying to go there. I search the room for some kind of weapon and realize I'm stuck.

"Midori, I'm sorry. Can we please talk?"

"Say what you gotta say through the door and then leave. I can't do this shit anymore."

"Midori, please. Let me sit down and talk to you."

"Sit your ass on the floor, if you feel the need to be sitting. I'm tired of this shit. How do you expect me to carry a baby under this kind of stress?"

"Baby, I know. Please, just let me explain."

I am now balled up in the bed again crying my heart out. Is this what happens when you get married out of necessity? I get my head together while I listen to him feed me more bullshit. I get my luggage set out of the closet. I begin with his shirts and start to neatly pack his shit up a piece at a time. I know he'll be mad about his clothes being folded, especially since he got everything starched so it would stay straight, but I don't care. I need some peace, by any means necessary.

I pack him enough stuff in four large suitcases to last him over a month. I take the liberty of cleaning all of his toiletries and stuff and packing them neatly in the outside pockets of his luggage so as not to mess up his clothes, and then I line up the bags at the bedroom door. He's been talking for so long I know he has to be hoarse, and I hope that was the case, because then maybe he'll shut up.

I'm confused and don't know what to do. One minute I want to be with Jaydah, and the next minute I want to be here. I just need time by myself to clear up my situation in my head.

Taking a deep breath, I go and open the bedroom door to find Ray sitting on the floor leaned against it. He falls backwards into the room, and I resist the urge to stomp him in his chest while he's flat on his back. Walking away from him, I climb back into the bed, gripping the spiked heel shoe I have under the covers tightly just in case I have to use it.

Ray looks from the luggage to me and back again with a puzzled look on his face. I knew he would think that was my shit packed up, and that's why I chose my luggage instead. He looks like he's trying to formulate a speech in his head on why I should stay, but little does he know, I'm not the one who'll be leaving.

"Midori, let's talk about this," he says, approaching the

bed. Seeing the fear in my face, he stops just shy of the foot of the bed and tries to reason with me. "Midori, please don't go. We can work this out. I've just been so tense lately, but we can fix this. I'll do whatever you want me to do."

"I'm not going anywhere, Ray."

"Then why do you have your bags packed?"

"That's your stuff. Just take it and go."

"But Midori, we need to—"

"Take your stuff and go, Ray. I need time."

"You are not going to do this to me," he says, coming around the bed and sitting on the side of me.

I grip the shoe even tighter, just in case I have to bust him in the eye or some shit. I know I can't beat him. But I'll die trying.

"Ray, we need some time apart."

"For how long?" He pleads with me with tears running down his face.

Normally the tears would make me re-think my decision, but this time around I can't take it. "I don't know, Ray. I just need to get my head together."

"Are you trying to divorce me, Midori? Huh?"

I don't know how to even answer the question because I'm not sure. I just know I don't want to be in the shit that I'm currently in. I'm tired of talking about it, tired of living in fear, and tired of having to watch my back. Ray is getting to be more abusive by the day, and what if the next time he actually kills me? Am I really willing to risk it?

"Ray, I just need some time to think."

"Why can't you think with me here? I'll stay in the guest room. I'll stay out of your way."

I think about it for a second, and I know he won't leave willingly. Maybe the guest room isn't a bad idea, but how long would he stay in there? Maybe if I lay down some ground rules or something. After all, he did buy this house. I can hear everything on me telling his ass to leave, but my mouth decides not to listen.

"Take all of that stuff with you then. You can stay, but you have to give me my space. I'll let you know when I'm ready to talk, so don't keep badgering me."

"But, Midori. I—"

"Or you can leave now."

He looks defeated, but decides to comply. I think partly because he knows I would change the shit out of those locks the very moment he rolls out.

It takes him two trips, but he gets the suitcases and moves into the guest room down the hall. I can hear him cursing because I folded his clothes up, but I don't care. As long as he stays his ass down there, I'm cool.

I know I want out. I just have to get my shit together so I can roll. The thing is, moving to Jaydah's would be a bad move too, and I know I have to fall back from her as well, if I truly want to get my shit together. She understands that, or so I hope. I'll just have to wait and see how it all goes down in the end.

If I Had My Way

Jaydah

I'm kicking it with Nevaeh again. Oh, and I know what you're thinking, but it's not like that. It's been a while since that night we glued her ass into her place, but I still want revenge. I want her to think we're cool, so when I really get her ass back, she will feel the sting. It's working too, because her simple ass went and dropped the restraining order and everything. I told her I had dropped mine too, and she never asked for any paperwork, so I just kept the lie going.

It took her a while to get over the stunt me and Midori pulled on her, though, because even though the door opens from the inside, Midori had glued the seal shut so that she couldn't open it up without tearing the door from its hinges. By the time maintenance showed up they had to knock the door down completely and rebuild the frame before putting another door up. She was even more pissed when she found out she would be getting charged for the damages. She couldn't leave until they finished, causing her to miss her flight and ultimately her photo shoot, and she was definitely pissed about that.

I miss the hell out of Midori, but I know what she has to do and I know I have to let her do it. So many nights I've wanted to call her up just to hear her voice, but I know that wouldn't be the right thing to do. She did ask me for space, and as her friend first, I owe her that.

I saw her husband at an art exhibit Nevaeh and I attended, and he smiled and spoke like he didn't know I was the one handling his wife for all these years. I guess because he was there with another woman, but she could have easily been family, so I stayed out of it.

They were giving out glasses of wine as we walked around, and I noticed the more wine he and his guest drank, the more free they got with their touching, confirming my initial thought. He's stepping out on Midori again. Nevaeh tried to be on some cuddled-up, holding-hands shit, but wasn't nothing going down. I really didn't get down with her like that, and it was strictly business.

I was moreso concentrating on staying close to Ray and his date, a couple of times snapping a few pictures of their asses in some compromising positions. Since this dude liked spreading pictures, I had something for his ass. I had something for Nevaeh as well, because I know she was the one who dipped on my stash and gave him the photos. It's funny because I had some of her in there also. I wonder why she didn't pull those out.

By the time we were done walking the exhibit, I got a chance to meet the host and stand around and talk for a while. She went by the name of Monica, no last name, and her art was breathtaking. She was cool as shit too, telling me that she was originally from Philly, but had moved to Atlanta a while ago. We got into a nice conversation, and I found out that she had a son here in Philly who she was trying to visit while she was here. I just assumed that her son was in college, even though she didn't look a day over thirty, but she cleared that right up by letting me know that her son was only two and that she was concerned because she hadn't heard from his guardians in a while.

She was so down-to-earth, and I found myself captivated by the shape of her mouth. She was petite and chocolate, just the way I like them. Family recognizes family, and something was telling me that she got down just like I did. I was truly enjoying our talk, until Nevaeh walked up with her jealous-ass self. I excused myself from Monica to go tend to her, but not before she slipped me her card and mouthed the words, "Call me." She was the shit, and I knew I might have to make it my business to visit the ATL, if that's how they were breeding them out there.

On the ride home, Nevaeh was acting all sour and shit, like something was wrong with her, and I tried my best to ignore her because I was anxious to download these pictures into my printer so I could show Midori when the time was right. Nevaeh was messing up my concentration though, sighing at every light and turning the volume on the radio up and down. I wanted to backhand her ass, but the last time I hit her I got locked up.

"Was she better looking than me?" Nevaeh finally asked me when I pulled up to my door.

I gave her a look that said, "Don't make me turn my damn car around and drive you back to Jersey," but she looked at me like she could care less what I thought.

"What are you talking about, Nevaeh? Is who better

looking than you?" I replied, trying to act like I didn't know exactly what she was talking about. You couldn't miss Monica in that room even if you were blind, but I didn't even know that chick to be sitting here getting in an argument about the shit.

"Oh, so now you gonna try to act like I'm the crazy one?" she said before getting out and slamming my car door so hard I thought my window would shatter.

I done told this chick about fucking with my whip, and she was still testing me. A small part of me believed that she liked getting her ass whipped in a kinky sort of way, but I wasn't in the mood tonight. I just got this car not too long ago, thanks to her wrecking my last one, and I didn't feel like going through any extra shit with her. I got out of my car and took a deep breath. I swear, I didn't feel like that shit.

"This is what we're going to do," I said to her, afterwards grabbing my belongings from the car so I wouldn't have to turn my back on this dizzy bitch if she decided to flip out.

"Nevaeh, get in your car and go home. Call me when you get there, okay?"

"I'm not leaving so you can call that bitch!" she said, storming toward the locked door of the building I lived in.

I was suddenly glad I had gotten my keys back from her because I hoped like hell I wouldn't have to bust her ass out here tonight.

My first instinct was to run after her, but I didn't. Instead I turned and got back in to my car and started it up. By the time she realized what I was doing, I was already backing my car out of my space and pulling off. I had to laugh as I watched her try to sprint up and catch my car, and she probably would have caught me if I was driving a little slower.

Why did I fuck with this chick? It wasn't the looks because, once again, even though I told her I'm tired of seeing her naked, she insisted on walking around with no damn clothes on. She was real catty-acting and always putting me through bullshit, yet I still fooled around with her. I must be a glutton for punishment.

Now, here I find myself in front of Midori and Ray's house just like I was back on Valentine's Day, looking through the binoculars that stayed in my glove compartment. Ray's car is parked in his usual spot, and I have the sudden urge to flatten his tires. I guess Midori stayed with him for the same reason I keep fooling around with Nevaeh—We don't know how to really part ways.

Digging in my pocket for my cell phone, I pull out Monica's number along with it. I toss the idea around in my mind on whether I should call her tonight, but I don't know if Nevaeh will be stalking me or if she will just peacefully go home. I know that idea is out the moment I look at my phone and saw all the missed calls I have from her. Driving off, I decide to give Monica a call anyway, just to see what she was up to.

She answers on the first ring, and I drive around aimlessly as we laugh and talk about everything. I stop to get gas and end up meeting her at this cute little restaurant named Tondalayah's that is known for having some good soul food. When we get there we are seated immediately, and Monica tells me it has been a while since she's been in there, but she had purchased the restaurant for one of her closest friends.

The owner isn't there, but we enjoy a delicious meal that is on the house, and the story she tells me about the situation with her son has me emotional.

I notice that her pink outfit matched her jeep perfectly. Even the interior is pink. We talk a little bit more outside of our cars before she goes on her way, promising to stay in touch.

I don't listen to Nevaeh's messages until I get safely in the house, not knowing if her crazy ass will jump out the bushes on me or some shit. She went from cursing me out, to apologizing, to cursing me out again, and honestly it doesn't faze me at all. I just know I am intrigued by this Monica chick and I know I have to get out to Atlanta as soon as possible. In the meantime, I take a second to download these pictures from my phone. I won't be using them right this second, but I know I will . . . eventually.

Silent Treatment

Midori

Surprisingly, Ray has been actually compromising, giving me space. All without a fight or anything. Not since that night when I packed up his shit has he said a word to me. By the time I come down in the morning he's already gone, and there's breakfast sitting on the table. Every morning I walk right past that shit because he might be trying to poison me on the low or something.

I've been getting a lot of prank calls also, and the few times I called back, the phone would ring at Mike's office. I chalk it up to Barbara's simple ass playing on my phone because she has nothing better to do, but Mike is actually still trying to be cool with me and Ray. I honestly didn't even have a problem with Mike, until I found out that he was in on that shit with his wife and my husband. For couples to swing, doesn't it take participation on both sides?

I wonder briefly about Jaydah. Did she ever finish her book up, and what happened with her and Nevaeh? I wouldn't be surprised if they were kicking it again, because

Jaydah is selfish like that, but I still miss her. The things she could do with her hands left me speechless. I know her book tour will be starting back up again soon too, and I'll miss those trips.

By the time I get to work, I have three messages from Ray. I hope he isn't calling with some begging shit, because I don't feel like it.

I wait until later in the afternoon to call him back, and by then he had called three more times. When my receptionist asked him if he wanted to leave a message, he would just say he'd call back. I honestly don't feel like talking to him about anything.

He calls again as I am leaving the job, and I mouth to my receptionist that I'm not there and don't even bother to wait for a response. Once outside, I hop in my car like someone is chasing me and speed off.

I'm curious about what Jaydah is doing and decide to stop over there before I go home to deal with Ray. Maybe we can sneak something in before I go home. It's been a while since I've been done right, and today I'm more than willing to return the favor.

I call her a couple of times on my way over, but she doesn't answer the phone. I decide to go ahead and pop up anyway because she may have been in her office writing, but I'm certain that I can sway her to have some fun for a little while. When I get there I see her new car parked in her designated space. She ended up getting that because her old car that Nevaeh messed up was too much to fix, so her insurance company wrote it off.

I dial her number once again after I get out of my car, and still get no answer. Maybe she's 'sleep or something, or maybe her ringer is off, because sometimes she does that when she's trying to concentrate. I say hello to her doorman and chat with him while I wait for the elevator to come.

I can smell all kinds of food cooking when I get off the elevator, and I know that's no one but Ms. Avery, Jaydah's neighbor, in there baking pies for church on Sunday. She would always send Jaydah down a pie every weekend, but I had to stop messing with that good home cooking because both our asses started getting a little heavy.

I knocked on Jaydah's door and waited. I could hear her laughing at something as she walked toward the door. I figure she must have had her ringer off because she's definitely home. She opens the door and peeks out, giving me a strange look that speaks volumes. I know my popping-up privileges were revoked a while ago, but I didn't think I would get this kind of greeting.

"Hey, call me back in about an hour. I got something I gotta do real fast," she says into the phone, never taking her eyes off me.

"Can I come in?" I ask her after an awkward silence. She has me just standing in the damn hallway, like I'm a stranger and shit. Is this the new Jaydah who is threatening to emerge this spring?

She opens the door hesitantly, like she really doesn't want me there, but I step in anyway because I'm determined to change her mind about me. She's more than likely still pissed about how things went down between us, and I should have been with her instead of Ray. I know this, but it's not like Ray and I are merely boyfriend and girlfriend. We are married, and walking away wouldn't be that sweet. I thought she got that, though.

"So what did I do to deserve this visit? It's been a while since you've been in my neck of the woods."

"It's been a while, I know. I was thinking about you, so I stopped by. I thought that was okay."

She's leaning against the door, her arms folded tight across her chest. She has on a cute little wife-beater that says SPOILED ROTTEN in rhinestones and a matching thong. She smells like she just got out of the shower, and everything looks nice and moisturized.

I tear my eyes away from her erect nipples to look in her face. Maybe I shouldn't be here, but I'm selfish and came to get what I want.

"Well, I wasn't doing anything really. Working on my next book, you know, trying to get it turned in."

"Cool. What do you want me to do? Come back or . . ." I don't know what to think. She's acting like she's truly moved on, and I'm hurt by it a little.

"No, you can chill since you're here, but do us both a favor and call before you come the next time."

She walks into her bedroom in front of me, and I take pleasure in watching her ass bounce with each step. She has that cranberry polish on her toes that I love so much, and she smells like my favorite scent, Almond Cookie from Carol's Daughter. Somebody must have taken a trip to New York without me.

I want to ask her who she was talking to on the phone before I walked up, but it really isn't any of my business. Besides all that, it was probably that damn Nevaeh. I take the liberty of scanning the place, and it doesn't look like anyone has moved in.

Jaydah smiles when she catches me searching, but she doesn't say anything.

I take my jacket off and hang it up on the back of her bedroom door, and make myself comfortable by removing my clothes down to my bra and panties and lying on the bed next to her.

She looks at me like she wants to say something, but instead she makes room for me on the bed before turning her attention back to her laptop.

I try to read over her shoulder, but I know she hates that, so I lay back on the bed with a pillow propped up under my head. I wish I had grabbed one of her ponytail holders before I lay down, because I don't feel like getting up. To compensate, I push my hair from under my neck and fan it out on the pillow. I watch her type away on her laptop for a few minutes, and decide I need to distract her so I can get what I want.

I didn't want to bother her, I swear, but when my hands began to travel down my stomach and to my throbbing clit, I know for sure that it would feel a lot better if it were her hands instead of mine. I want her to strap up with my favorite toy and do to me what she did to make me fall for her in the first place. I wonder briefly if she had used it on Nevaeh, but I don't have the heart to ask.

Leaning over, I kiss her on her shoulder just as she is pushing the save icon on the screen. I remember her telling me one time that she did that often while she was writing, just in case something happened along the way. After she clicks the button, I close the computer completely and motion for her to turn on her back.

She looks at me like I'm crazy at first, but after securing her laptop on the nightstand next to the bed she obliges and turns over for me.

I don't rush. I take my time kissing the smooth skin on her stomach, noticing that she is getting a little thick, but it's in all the right places. Normally she would have taken off her shirt and panties, but I guess she's making me work for it tonight.

I move up and press my body against hers, sucking and biting her nipples through the fabric of her shirt, welcoming the feel of her legs wrapped around me. I move up more, so loving the feel of her warmth against my pelvis, and I want to remove both of our panties so I can feel her slickness on me.

Pushing her shirt up, I press her breasts together and tease her nipples until a moan escapes her lips. We are grinding in a slow motion, and I know enough to know that her clit is pressed against my pelvis and giving her all kinds of pleasure. My hands roam her body freely, easily remembering every nook and cranny that makes her a woman.

I slide down her body, trailing kisses along the way, until I get to her well-kept triangle, the heat a welcome feeling against my face.

Jaydah has her legs up and out in a perfect *V*, and I know her clit is pulsating, waiting for me to touch it. I move her thong to the side and stick my tongue out like I'm going to lick an ice cream cone and dip my tongue into her slit. Her body tenses up and relaxes when I take her clit into my mouth and suck on it the way she likes it. I'm hoping she'll come quickly.

I'm stirring up my own juices, my middle finger racing back and forth across my clit. I can't wait to feel my toy inside me again. I put everything I have into pleasing her, but I'm distracted by her cell phone ringing.

She hears it too, because she swings her legs over around my head and gets up from the bed to answer it.

When she does, a smile spreads across her face a mile

wide. Whoever is on that phone must be special, because I've only known her to smile like that when she was talking to me. She takes the call outside the room and I can hear her laughing.

When I look at the clock, an hour has passed since I'd gotten there. She must be talking to whomever she instructed to call back. I'm salty as shit about this, but I hope she'll end her call so we can finish. No sooner than the thought pops in my head, she comes back in the room.

"Hey, listen," she begins as she scoops her laptop up from the table and cradles it in her arms. "We're going to have to hook up another time. I need to take this call. Let yourself out, okay?"

She doesn't bother to wait until I answer. She turns back around and goes into the living room.

I'm so fucking mad, I'm seeing red. I start to just go in there and finish what I was doing, but I get dressed instead. When I come out into the living room, she's laid back on the couch with her feet kicked up, smiling and shit. I want to hurt her real bad, but I keep it moving.

When she looks up, she holds her hand over the mouthpiece on her flip phone and mouths, "We will talk soon."

I slam the door so hard, I hope her pictures fell off the damn wall. It doesn't seem to faze her, because I can still hear her laughing in her phone conversation. I shouldn't have come over here, and as I drive home I hope I don't have no mess to clean up there. Hopefully Ray's ass is still at the office and I can just go up to my room.

Phone Sex

Jaydah

"So did you find them?" I ask Monica about the situation concerning her son.

Apparently, the couple who adopted her son are missing in action, and she was trying to get to the bottom of the situation. They couldn't be found, and that was against the contract agreement they had set up when she left town. Monica never really got into exactly how she came to give up her son and the circumstances behind how he was conceived, but something tells me she got into some shit when she was here, and that was the reason why she rolled out.

I've learned a lot about Monica since I met her at the art exhibition a few days ago. She was originally from Philly, living right in the neighborhood I grew up in. She said she was down here for the art exhibit she sponsored once a year for molested children and to visit some guy she's messing around with who plays for the Eagles, but they never got a chance to hook up.

* * *

I liked her conversation though. She's greedy just like I am, wanting enjoyment from both sexes, but enjoying women more. We agree that I will make a trip down there, and that will be cool, because I'll just have my publicist set me up some signings during my visit.

"You should put me in one of your books. I guarantee my life story would be a best-seller." She laughs into the phone.

It would be interesting to pick her brain, but do I really want to know that much about her?

"Let me think about it," I tell her as we continue our conversation. I know that what she would have to say would determine how long my ass stuck around.

"So what's your story? What masks are you hiding behind?" Monica asks me in an inquisitive voice.

I don't know how much I should share with her but figure, how much could I lose? Just dealing with Nevaeh is a story within itself, and I need a damn laugh real fast.

I know Midori was mad about having to leave. I'm not going to lie to you, I miss the way she could just touch me with just her pinky finger and make my body go into convulsions. I was on my way to a nice orgasm too when the phone rang.

That hour went fast, and I didn't think Monica would be calling me right back, but in a way I was glad she did. If Midori was successful in making me cum, I would have been stuck again. That thought doesn't stop me from fingering my pussy while I talk to Monica on the phone.

I abandon my laptop to the coffee table, and I'm trying to forget what Midori did to me, but the slickness between my legs won't let me.

"Jaydah, what are you doing?" Monica asks me for maybe the third time.

I didn't hear her the first two obviously, and decide to play devil's advocate just to see where her head is at.

"My clit is begging for attention," I respond in a breathy voice while I press it between my thumb and forefinger.

"Is that so? Do you have your panties off?" she asks, sounding like she's trying to get comfortable.

"Yeah," I say, slipping out of my thong in record time.

"Okay, I want you to follow me and do as I tell you. Take your shirt off if you have one on. I want you completely naked like me."

Telling her to hold on, I pull my wife-beater over my head, the cool air in my drafty condo covering me like a second skin. I'm so comfortable on the couch that I don't want to move to turn the heat up. Besides, I know that by the time this conversation is over I'll be on fire!

"Hello?" I say into the phone after I make myself comfortable again on the couch.

"Don't get scared now." Monica laughs into the phone in a sexy sort of way.

I give her a slightly nervous laugh in return, puzzled by why I am so tense. I've done this plenty of times with Midori and Nevaeh, so what's so different now?

"I ain't never scared. Trust and believe. Now let's get this thing started."

I chance a glance at the clock and see that it was almost eight o'clock. I guess I can miss an episode of *American Idol* for a possible orgasm. I like Monica's style, and I know, if we ever hook up on this level, it will be off the chain. It appears that both of us like to be the dominant one, and I'd like to see how it plays out.

"Put one leg on the back of the couch and one on the floor. Part your lips and stick your finger in your mouth."

I'm excited already and take my time doing what she said. I close my eyes to pretend that she was right here doing it herself, but to my surprise I don't see Monica when I close my eyes. I see Midori.

"Now part your lower lips and rub your finger across your clit in a steady rhythm. Squeeze it between your fingers and tug on it a little bit," Monica moans into the phone, turning me the hell on.

My clit piercing feels slick from my juices, and the slight tugging on it had my walls pulsating. I wish for a quick second that we had web cams or some shit, so I can watch it go down.

"Rest the phone between your ear and your shoulder and use your free hand to fondle your nipples. Put one in your mouth."

All of this was said just above a whisper, and I am losing my damn mind. My entire body tingles, and I break out in a sweat, despite the chilly temperature in my condo. I wish I had brought a toy before I came in here, but I don't want to get up, because it's feeling too good.

"You wanna cum, don't you?" Monica says into the phone seductively.

I think I've lost my voice for a second because, I swear, I can't fix my mouth to talk.

"Yes, I wanna cum."

"You better not," she says with force.

That shit just made me even hotter, and I don't know how long I'll be able to hold it.

"Pull your fingers out and taste yourself. Tell me what you taste like."

This chick is a freak. I might have to get my ass down to At-lanta sooner than I thought. I close my eyes again, wishing I was with her, but all I see is Midori. I pop my eyes back open, still trying to control my orgasm.

"Tell me what you taste."

Just as I am getting ready to answer her, my other line clicks. I put my hand back down and pull on my clit ring, trying to ignore it, and I'm getting pissed because it is messing up my flow. My orgasm is so close.

"Don't click over. Cum for me. Tell me when you cum."

I take a quick look at the screen on my phone and see that it is Nevaeh. She always picks the most inopportune times to want to call or show the hell up. I know that if I don't take the call she'll just keep calling back, but I am willing to chance that. I just want to get this nut out.

"Can I cum now?"

"Yeah, cum with me. Cum with me, Jaydah . . ."

At that moment the phone clicks again, but my entire body is convulsing and I am moaning at the top of my lungs. Usually I am the one controlling this kind of situation, but it feels good and different to be the one controlled. I have a feeling that this situation with Monica is going to work out just fine.

"Feel good?" Monica asks, a slight giggle in her voice.

Shit, I'm winded. "Yeah, definitely felt good," I reply while I tried to catch my breath.

My other line clicks once again, and the look on my face changes from bliss to frustration.

"Answer your other line. I'm going to wash my hands and get something to eat. Give me a call later if you're still up."

"I'll do that. Just answer the phone."

Instead of clicking over, I hang up the phone completely and do the same thing. Orgasms definitely make you hungry, and I am famished. I take the time to rinse off over the sink really quickly and I put on my nightgown before looking for something to eat.

My phone rings again, and this time I answer it.

Back Then, Back When

Midori

When I get home I'm still pissed at Jaydah. I can't believe I let her play me like that. What made me go over there anyway? I should have just called my damn husband back to see what he wanted. Maybe that would have deterred me from even thinking about her. Ray's car is in the driveway when I get there, and I hope for his sake he doesn't try to start an argument. The way I'm feeling right now, he'll get cut if he says something sideways out his mouth tonight.

Walking into the house, I'm greeted by rose petals that lead to the kitchen. With the mood I'm in, I'm tempted to shoot right past them and go up the steps, but a part of me wants to make sure he ain't have some other bitch in my kitchen. Men are stupid like that sometimes.

I am pleasantly surprised to find a lobster dinner waiting. He pulled out the candles and everything. I don't smell any Pine-Sol, so I guess he isn't trying to make it obvious he is going to poison me. He smiles at me from his spot at the table, and I frown in return, not in the mood for this shit.

"What's this all about, Ray?" I ask from the kitchen door, not bothering to move any closer.

"It's our wedding anniversary. Did you forget?" he asks, a look of shock on his face.

I look over at the calendar that was on the refrigerator, and sure enough he has our wedding anniversary circled in a red marker. I've been so busy walking straight past breakfast that I never noticed it. At that same moment I notice a gift box on the table and I feel like shit. I'm still hesitant to sit down, and Ray still has a loving smile on his face.

After a few awkward minutes he gets up from his chair and comes to me, planting a soft kiss on my lips. My body sways a little on contact, and I feel horrible because I still have Jaydah on my lips. He doesn't act as if he smells or tastes anything different, so I keep my damn mouth shut and take my seat. He ushers me over to my seat and makes sure I'm pushed close enough to the table comfortably.

"How was your day, honey?" Ray asks after he takes his seat across from me.

"It was cool. A typical day at the office," I reply, not making eye contact. I feel guilty as hell, but I don't know why. Didn't he cheat on me as well?

"You must have been extra busy. I have been calling you all day."

"Yeah, it was one of those days," I say, looking down at my plate. "Umm, do you mind if I shower first? I would like to go and change into something more comfortable."

"If you go up now, you'll ruin my surprise. We have time for all that. Just enjoy your dinner."

He places a steamed lobster tail in front of me along with mixed veggies and a small dish of melted butter. I notice that he pulls out the bottle of champagne we got as a gift for our wedding from Mike and Barbara. Knowing Ray, he probably forgot that detail, but I still give him an A for effort. I wait for him to take a few bites of his dinner before I decide it's safe to eat mine.

We chat a little bit, and I find myself laughing at some of the memories we share. I guess us being together hasn't been all bad. At some point during dinner we end up sitting next to each other and feeding each other the remaining lobster tails that were left in the steamer. He licks butter from my fingers, and I taste the champagne from the corner of his mouth, easing him into a kiss. It's been ages since I've felt like this, and in all honesty I didn't think we had any romance left in our relationship.

Still kissing, Ray lifts me up from the chair and carries me upstairs to the room we used to share. I haven't let him back in since I told him to roll out, and for the first time I regret ever making that decision. I have to ask Ray to put me down and run back downstairs to get my pocketbook so I can unlock the bedroom door. A day after I first gave him the boot I went and replaced the doorknob so he wouldn't be able to come in while I was here, or gone for that matter.

When I open the door, there are rose petals everywhere. The Jacuzzi is filled and there is a bottle of champagne resting on ice. When I turn and look at him, he gives me a weak smile.

"I climbed through the window. I wanted it to be a surprise."

I can't say a word. I just let it be what it is.

He walks up to me with the gift box that I totally forgot was on the table. I take a seat on the bed, and he kneels in front of me. For some reason I start sweating, and I feel bad that I forgot all about today and didn't even get him a gift. *I'll have to make it up to him tomorrow.*

"Midori, I'm sorry for everything. Do you believe me?"

"Yeah, I believe you."

He opens the box to reveal a beautiful diamond tennis bracelet. The underside is engraved with our names and wedding date in script. That just makes me feel worse. After the bracelet is secured on my wrist, he begins to unbutton my shirt and take my clothes off.

"I don't want to see you in anything but your wedding ring and that bracelet."

I don't have time to protest, and within seconds I'm naked and my husband is carrying me to the Jacuzzi.

He sets me down gently in the tub, and after taking a few seconds to get undressed, he gets in himself. He pulls me on top of him, and when my clit brushes against his erection, my body tenses up. He pulls my face toward his and embraces me, kissing me on my nose then my lips.

I, in the meantime, rub the heat and stickiness from my pussy up and down the length of him, avoiding the head so he can't enter me yet.

He has his hands all over me. It's been a long time since I've felt close to him, and I wonder briefly if, like a few months back, we are thinking about the same person. I wonder if Jaydah would have agreed to a threesome with him. I don't want to share her with anyone, but apparently she already has someone in mind.

I lean back and allow Ray to cater to my breasts, while I rock back and forth on his lap, thinking about the last time Jaydah and I got together before all the bullshit. Barbara's naked ass pops in my head for a split second, and I wonder why Mike ever agreed to share his wife in the first place.

"Midori, what's wrong?" Ray asks me, stopping what he is doing to look me in the face.

"Nothing's wrong. Why you ask me that?" I reply, blushing a little, like he could read my thoughts.

"You just seem kind of distant. Like you're not really into this," he says, a concerned look on his face.

I feel bad about having to lie, but on the real, I'm ready to get out of the tub and lay in the bed. I can feel his erection going down, and that makes me feel worse.

"Babe, I'm good. I want you to turn me out like you used to."

That puts a smile on his face, and he jumps right back to attention. His hands and tongue reach places on my body that I didn't even know existed, but I have to say that my mind isn't all the way there. I want shit to go back to the way it used to be when I could still knock Ray off and the very next day be on my way to Virginia Beach with Jaydah on her book tour. I also have to play it safe because after that initial Depo-Provera shot I never went back, and sadly if I do pop up pregnant I'll be at the women's center flushing it down the river.

"Lift up a little bit," Ray says, already pushing my body up and pulling me back down.

I can't tell my husband to put on a condom, and I'm not sure if he is going to be quick like he normally is, or if he is going to ride the night out, so I can't time it. All I can do is hope the damn shot worked.

I hold on to his shoulders and bounce up and down, pretending like I am bouncing on me and Jaydah's favorite toy. I close my eyes and try to pretend that he is Jaydah, but his dick has a pulse that hers doesn't. He also doesn't have her soft curves and full breasts.

At this point I'm working overtime to get him to cum, but he decides to stand up in the tub and wrap my legs around him so he can step out. I hope like hell that his ass won't slide on this floor or we will both go down, and with him still inside of me that wouldn't be a good thing.

He smashes my body up against the wall and begins drilling me all crazy. He has my breasts bouncing all over the place, and my pussy is making this slurping sound as he moves in and out. He's doing the damn thing to me, and this is the one position Jaydah couldn't put me in. After all, we were both women. The fact that she would prop me up on her kitchen counter and get up on the barstool and do the damn thing to me wasn't lost on me, though. True, there were a few positions, as women, we couldn't conquer, but she did what she did very well.

He took me from the wall to the dresser, knocking all of my shit on the floor so he can make room for my ass. I'm trying to catch his rhythm, but by the time I get it together, he has already grabbed a hold of me and busted off inside me for the first of a few times that night.

At one point he has me hanging off the bed practically upside down, and I know that in this position his sperm has a good chance of traveling upward and impregnating me, so I pray to God once again that Depo shot works.

He won't stay off of me. Even after we're settled on the bed and I decide to let him stay in the room with me, he won't go to sleep. Every time I doze off, he's right back in me.

Shit, by the morning I'm sore as hell, and he's still trying to get it. Is this what I have to look forward to?

Something is telling me that he's trying to make sure, if nothing else, that I am pregnant, but I don't feed much into it. Once I get to work I'll be getting me another shot, and I make a mental note to see about one of those morning-after pills as well. He isn't going to catch me ass out like that. If I want to roll, I don't need a child making me have to stay.

Addicted

Jaydah

"What's up, Nevaeh?"

"You tell me. I've been calling you for the last half hour. You got me standing out here in the cold."

"Correction, you got *yourself* standing out in the cold. You should have called before you came over."

I made the hell out of this turkey sandwich, and I'm enjoying it. I know once I get a hold of Monica it will be on. I don't feel like dealing with Nevaeh tonight, not after that last phone conversation. But she was already here, so I went ahead and buzzed her in after making her wait an additional ten minutes.

She arrived at my door in a black trench coat. Underneath she wore a lace bra and panty set, compliments of Vicky's with red stiletto heels to match. Her toes were painted the same fire engine red, and so were her lips.

I wasn't even impressed. I'd seen Midori dressed like that millions of times. Only now, I am picturing Monica dressed like that in the middle of my bedroom, instead of her.

While Nevaeh flaunts back and forth in front of me, I flip through the pictures I have in my phone of Ray and his mystery woman at the art exhibition. I have them already printed out and in an envelope ready to send them to Midori. I just haven't decided if I will send them out yet. I mean, who am I to wreck a happy home?

And why can't I get this Monica chick off my mind? Outside of spending a few hours with her when she was here and some bomb-ass phone sex, what else is there? Now, I'm not going to hold you, Monica has her shit together. In the looks department, she is killing the game, and her conversation left me dripping wet, but I need to know more about her. What's this situation with her son that she isn't spilling the beans about? By looking at her, you would never guess she carried a child with such a petite, tight frame.

Right after we hung up, she sent me a picture of her in her bra and panties to my phone, and I saw that she has Janet Jackson abs when she did the "I Get Lonely" video. I know she had to have worked hard to snap back to that.

"Oh, so you're just going to ignore me, huh?" Nevaeh pouted.

That pout used to have me stuck, but now I could care less. I'm still not over the fact that she wrecked my ride, so you know how that goes.

Instead of responding to Nevaeh, I pick up my laptop and power it up so I can get back to working on my book. I'm almost done, short only about forty pages or so, and I hope to get it done within the next couple of days. I have another book I want to jump right into, but I can't do that until I finish up this shit here.

"Jaydah, I could have stayed home," she says to me as she flops down next to me on the bed.

I look at her out the corner of my eye to see if she is serious. Did I invite her here? I have to ask just in case I missed something.

"Did I invite you here?"

"No, you didn't, but since we've gotten back together, we haven't spent any time. You messing with that Midori chick again or something?"

"Here we go again." I sigh into my laptop, placing my head on the keyboard momentarily before lifting my head to continue typing. When does the jealousy bullshit stop?

"Yeah, here we go again," she says, jumping up from the bed and throwing her hands on her hips. "If you don't want me here, just say so."

I roll over onto my back, so I can get a good look at her. I want to say some grimy shit to her, but I just got my new car, and this time I'll have to chop her ass up in little pieces and hide her in the deep freezer or some shit. I'm not in the mood to be sitting back up in jail.

"So, is this the bullshit I have to go through with you every single time? This is exactly the reason why I'm taking my ass to Atlanta."

She freezes in place and gives me a look that resembles a deer caught in headlights.

My face probably resembles that very same look for a few seconds, but I recover quickly, not believing I said that shit out loud. I mean, Monica and I talked about it, but I never said that I would definitely go until now. Fuck it, why not? At the very least, I can sell some books while I'm down there.

"You're moving to Atlanta?"

I don't answer at first because I don't know if I want her to believe that I was going to stay, or be truthful and tell her it's just a visit. But if I say I'm visiting for business she'll want to go, and if she couldn't go, she would want a hotel number, and it was already getting to be too much. I should be a smart ass and give her Monica's number, but I don't know what kind of chick Monica is, and I don't feel like any nonsense this early in the game when I could cum from just a phone conversation.

"I'm not sure. I'll see once I get there."

"Then what am I supposed to do?"

Frustration creeps up in my voice, and I'm about to act a damn fool. "What do you mean what are you going to do? Live in your damn condo where you been at."

I never even considered moving to Atlanta, but if that's an out from dealing with Nevaeh's ass, I might just consider it and see what Hotlanta has to offer. But what about Midori?

She looks like she's going to cry, so I soften my voice up a little. When we first hooked up, I'm not going to lie to you, I enjoyed her smothering me and all the attention she gave me. Now, I didn't really like it, but people don't just change overnight. I came at her with a different approach.

"Nevaeh, listen, I'm sorry about that, okay? I'm visiting Atlanta to see what it's about. I also have book signings set up down there, so I haven't decided if I'm going to stay or not. I'm just going to chill for a few days to see what's really good."

"But you're coming back, right?" she asks in a scared voice, like she knows I'm not.

"Yeah, I'll be back. I've never been down there. I'm just going to see if I like it."

"And when are you leaving?"

"Not sure yet."

"But you just said you had book signings scheduled. When is that?"

"Nevaeh, honestly," I reply with frustration again. She didn't even get a chance to let me finish.

"Okay, Jaydah. Can we just lie down and cuddle for a while? I just want to be held."

I let her simple ass get in the bed after setting my laptop on the nightstand, and we spoon while I watch television. I need to finish my damn book, but it's cool, because her ass will be out in the morning.

I end up closing my eyes by the time the news comes on, and all I can do is think about going to Atlanta and chilling with Monica. She said she had a sister who was cool as hell too, named Yolanda, so I can't wait to hang out with her as well. She was telling me about this club called Masquerade, where all the ballers hang out, so we'll see.

By the morning, Nevaeh is already gone. When I get in the kitchen I see she left a note on the fridge letting me know she'll be back later. Now, didn't I just tell her I need some space? I snatch the note off the door and toss it in the garbage, making a mental note to call her before I step out.

Hopping in the shower real quick, I handle my business before my mind and my hands started roaming. I just have some quick things I need to do today, and then I'll be back in front of my computer. I'm distracted easily, and talking to Monica is proving itself to be a major distraction, so I'll have to fall back from her for a second too, if I want to get this book in on time.

Once I get to my car, my phone starts ringing off the hook. To my surprise it's Midori. I start to let her ass go straight to voice mail too, but she has to be calling because something happened. Do I really want to know? I pick up the phone before I can make up my mind.

"Hey, Midori, wassup?"

"What are you doing later?"

"Writing, trying to get my book finished up," I reply, letting her know that I'm not in the mood for any company. That reminds me to call Nevaeh, so her ass won't show up either.

"Oh, okay. I'm at work. I just called to see if I could stop by later, you know, just to talk. It's been a while since we've talked, and I could really use your shoulder right now."

I have to think hard on this because, do I really want to be in her business? I have my own shit going on, and I don't feel like it right now.

"Well, I'm doing a little running around right now. What time did you want to come by?"

"Is six okay?"

"Yeah, six is cool."

"Okay, I'll pick up some dinner on the way."

We end our call, and I'm hoping she won't be there long enough to have dinner. Driving out of my lot and to the expressway, I make a mental checklist for things I need to pack for my trip. Something is telling me that Monica has some shit up her sleeve that will have my head spinning, but I have a few tricks as well. My first stop will be Fetish down on Fourth and Bainbridge. They always have some good stuff.

Please Don't Go

Midori

It's been a busy day at the office, but I make time to take a pregnancy test before I do anything else. It's still in my pocket as a matter of fact. Something about it just doesn't seem right. I don't know where the guilt's coming from, and I'm not sure I even want to figure it out.

I make myself a note to check back on it after I'm done with my morning patients, but I still want a sample sent off because a lot of times the traditional stick tests aren't accurate and blood is needed to get results that can be trusted. I copped one of those morning-after pills too, but for whatever reason I didn't take it right away.

Could it be that abortion I never told Ray about back in 2005? Jaydah took me over to this spot in Jersey that she knew about, so I wouldn't have to do it over here in Philly. They didn't even ask for identification. I just paid my three hundred, got up on the table, and the machine did its work. The only thing is, I bled so much from it that I ended up in the emergency room over there as well. (Jaydah had book signings in Newark, we had a hotel room.) I was bleeding so much, I could barely stand, and when I went to the ER, they had to perform a second abortion because the guy I went to didn't remove all of the tissue he was supposed to.

We were so scared because I was passing blood clots the size of tangerines, and the blood was so heavy, I was doubling up and changing soiled sanitary napkins every hour. It was horrible, and I remember Jaydah holding my wilted body in her arms while I cried and cried, not knowing what I should do.

She rubbed my back and helped me in the bathroom because I was so weak. We ended up staying over there for a week, until I was able to get my head on straight, and it was a secret that we never spoke of again. She did her book signings, but she called me every half hour she was away from the room, to check on me. That's when I knew she really loved me.

I show up at Jaydah's exactly at six. Before I got there I stopped past Pier 22, a little seafood restaurant in South Philly, and got her the Fisherman's Platter she loves so much. I also got a pound of extra large shrimp and two pounds of crab legs so we can feast. Jaydah loved some seafood.

I'm a little nervous when I get there, and when she opens the door to let me in, I don't know how long I'll be able to contain myself. For whatever reason, Jaydah just never wore real clothes in the house. I always laughed because, every time I asked her why she was never dressed, she'd say that clothes were for outside. It's those quirky kind of things that make her unique. She has on a red thong and bra set, and she smells freshly showered.

I didn't come here to get into nothing, but I certainly won't object if something pops off.

"I bought all of your favorites. I know how much you love seafood," I say to her, setting the bags down on the counter.

She signals that she'll be right back, and at the moment I notice that she's on the phone. She gives me a quick smile and went and sat on her bed, leaving me in the kitchen.

I start unpacking the food and getting out plates and stuff so we can eat when I heard her laughing into the phone. Who is she talking to that has her all giggling and shit? I creep up by the door to listen to what she's talking about. Chancing a glance into her room, I see her lying on her back in the bed with her legs crossed while she plays with her hair and smiles on the phone. Whoever she's talking to is the bomb, apparently.

"So you can't find them?" she asks, serious all of a sudden.

I don't want to get caught in the hallway, and know I should get back to the kitchen, but this is getting too good. Whomever she was talking to responds, and I can feel the mood get almost sad.

"So when are you going to come here? I can help you find him."

I walk away at that point because, whatever it is, I really don't want to know about it. I have my own shit, and I don't feel like hearing anyone else's problems.

She comes out of the room a few minutes later, and I act like I didn't hear anything that was said. She sits down across from me and begins putting shrimp on her plate from out of the containers.

"If I wanted you in my conversation, I would have had it right here," she says to me with obvious agitation on her face.

I'm shocked, but I strain to not show it on my face. Maybe she heard my footsteps or something as I approached the door. I don't bother to respond, I simply continue to eat my food.

The silence is awkward, and I think for a second that maybe I should just leave. It's obvious that she has more pressing shit to deal with than me being here.

"Okay, so I'm going to go. Maybe I'll call you later," I say, getting up to clear my plate.

"So you came here for what exactly? To feed me?" Jaydah responds in a sarcastic voice followed by a laugh, as she continues to peel and eat her shrimp.

"I came here to talk to my friend. I came here because I thought we still at least had that."

How could I have been so damn stupid? What made me think after all this time that I was welcome over here? Ever since Valentine's Day we've been going through the motions, and my life has been a damn wreck. If it isn't Jaydah, it's Ray, and I'm so damn tired of both their asses.

Instead of arguing with her, I walk around her and back into the living room to get my shit so I can bounce. I could have done without this bullshit, and I wasted my damn money. I go to throw my coat on, and Jaydah is behind me pulling it the other way.

"Midori, don't leave. I'm just being a bitch, I'm sorry. Stay and have dinner with me. Besides, I have some things I want to discuss with you."

I turn to look at her to make sure she's sincere. I have my own problems, and I thought, if no one else, I could come to her and talk. We have a couple of years under our belt, and I can't see a few lies ending all the good.

I put my bag down and walk back to the kitchen, grabbing another plate. I hate her sometimes, but at the very same time there are so many things that keep me here.

We sit at the table in silence, eating our food. I want to ask her what it was she wanted to talk about, but I don't want to appear anxious. Besides, I know I can't stay here but for so long before Ray sends the dogs out to look for me.

We finish what we're going to eat of our meal, and she tells me that she has to grab something from her office, and she'll meet me in the living room.

I'm nervous. Why? Not sure, but whatever it is, I'd rather know now, so I can deal with it while I have the heart.

She comes back into the living room with a manila envelope. I wish for a second I could see through it.

"So, in a few days I'll be going down to Atlanta. I have some book signings lined up for a couple days. I'll be looking around at some other stuff too. I'm thinking about relocating out that way."

"That's perfect. I mean, the trip. I have a conference down there over the weekend. Maybe we can fly out together and share a room?" I say, totally avoiding the fact that she said she might be leaving me here. I smile, although on the inside I'm ready to bust her in her damn face.

"Actually I'm staying with a friend of mine down there, but I'll definitely hit you up when I get back."

"Oh, okay. Well, do that."

She's dismissing me. I can't believe that after all the break-up to make-up she is really about to end it for good. I put my head down for a second, but smile when I look at her. We've had some good times, that's all that really matters. I can only hope that we can walk away from all of this with at least a friendship and on good terms. I just hope she isn't leaving me for that model bitch.

"So, what else did you want to discuss?" I ask, not really wanting to know.

I don't feel like any more surprises, and I want to share the results of my pregnancy test with her because I don't know what my next step should be. Ray caught me slipping, and his little anniversary surprise worked. I'm just not sure if I should let him know or not.

"I was out at an art exhibit with a friend of mine," she says hesitantly.

This must be really bad. I urge her to continue, bracing myself for the news.

"Okay, so what happened there? You purchased a new painting or something?" I ask, allowing a laugh to escape from my throat, although I feel the exact opposite of what a laugh really means.

She looks like it hurts her to even have to say anything to me, but I just need to hear it straight. I want to grab her by her shoulders and scream at the top of my lungs for her to say what it is, but I play it cool. Whatever it is, I need to be able to handle it.

She doesn't say a word. She just pulls out the contents of the envelope.

Apparently Ray and Barbara are still seeing each other. I take the pictures from her hands, so I can look at them closer. They were all over each other, and it looks like they had been drinking. I'm so mad, I can't even drop a tear if I wanted to. I just want to hurt somebody. That, in a nut-shell, determines what I needed to do about my situation now.

"They were at the exhibit. I don't know who the woman is, I just knew she wasn't you. I hope these help your situa-tion."

Once again I'm speechless. I'll have to thank her at a later date. Right now I have to go dig up in Ray's ass right fast. I put my coat on and grab my bag. She walks me to the door and embraces me in a tight hug. I can feel that it hurt her to have to tell me about my husband, but I'm glad it came from her and not someone from my office.

"Jaydah, thanks for everything. I hope after all this we can at least remain friends."

"Forever. Just go handle your business."

I give her a kiss on the cheek and roll out.

I'm busting a hundred all the way home because I have a bone to pick with Mr. Raymond Hunter. I'm glad to see that his car is in the driveway. I resist the urge to flatten his damn tires as I come to a screeching halt and race into the house.

I find my loving husband in the kitchen cooking din-ner. He looks like he's happy to see me, but the feeling isn't mutual. I don't say a word, I just set the pictures on the table and walk away.

Once I get upstairs I begin packing a bag. Ray comes and stands at the door, trying to plead his case, but it falls on deaf ears. I have to do what I have to do for me.

He fights me tooth and nail all the way to the car, and I end up leaving all the shit I packed in the house and getting in my car and rolling out.

I start to go back to Jaydah's but decide against it. Instead I call Sprint to change my number, then I check into a hotel. I'll be cool. I'll handle everything when I get back from Atlanta.

Like You'll Never See Me Again

Jaydah

I'm at the airport at seven in the morning waiting for my flight. I already had my luggage checked in and am enjoying a pretzel from Auntie Anne's. It's Valentine's Day weekend, and to think just a year ago I was sitting outside my ex-lover's house peering at her through binoculars. I have a feeling things would be a lot different with Monica, though. She just seems a lot more put together. Nothing's official, but I have to smile at the thought of using all the new toys I have packed in my luggage.

I decided to stay at her house for two weeks instead of four days. She has to come back to Philly anyway to handle some issues with her son. She still hasn't told me the entire situation, but from what I understand, she gave her son up for adoption, but the couple supposedly dipped out on her, and her support checks are being returned. I don't even feel like that kind of drama, but I'll enjoy her ass for the moment.

We've been talking all morning, and she said she would have a car pick me up from the airport. I can't wait to see her.

I have about ten minutes before my flight left, so I decide to go ahead and use the bathroom so I won't have to on the plane. I make it quick because I know on Southwest they call you by sections, and I don't want to miss my call.

When I get out front I grab my carry-on bag and get in line. The woman standing in front of me is the shit from behind. She has curves like, *"Damn,"* and her wrap is flowing. I can hear her telling someone that she'll meet them in Atlanta, and her voice sounds familiar.

I clear my throat to see if she will turn around, and to my surprise Midori and I come face to face.

"Hey, what are you doing here?" She smiles at me in surprise.

I return the smile as well. "On my way to Atlanta."

"So am I. Where are you sitting?"

"14A," I respond as I straighten my bag up on my shoulder.

"I'm in 14B. This is too funny."

"That's cool. We can talk while we ride."

I help Midori with her bag, and once we get settled, she grabs my hand and intertwines her fingers between mine like we always did when we sat next to each other. For the first time in a while she seems genuinely happy, but I don't ask why. I'm just happy to see her smile again.

We both get quiet like we usually do when the plane begins to ascend, and I pray silently for traveling mercy as we make our way to the ATL.

It's good seeing Midori, and I'd take her back in a heart-beat under different circumstances. We chat like old friends, and I miss her like you wouldn't believe.

Once the plane lands and we get our luggage, we hug in the airport and promise to hook up once we get back to Philly. I go ahead and get in the car Monica had arranged for me, and as I dig in my pocket for my cell phone, I pull out a piece of paper as well. It had Midori's name on it, but the phone number was different. I smile before I tear it to shreds, not bothering to enter it in my phone. I am here to see what Atlanta has to offer. But if it's meant to be, we'll meet up again. Maybe then we'll be right for each other.

SNEAK PREVIEW OF

by

ANNA J.

Coming in September 2009

Joey Street

Wrong Place at the Wrong Time

Friday, 3:00 am

"**M**an, I know you ain't getting scared now. All we gotta do is walk in there and take the money. It's only two of 'em in there, so it'll be a piece of cake," Bunz said to me as we blazed an *L* in the parked car we were sitting in across the street from the African hair braiding shop on the corner of Fortieth and Lancaster Avenue.

It was three o'clock in the damn morning, and I knew my girl Shanyce was gonna be mad as shit when I got home, but I had to get this paper. We'd been scouting this place for like two weeks now, and figured that Marie's African Hair Braiding Shop was getting mad paper. I saw the heavyset sista with the cute face walk into the shop around seven-thirty that night, and I thought for sure they were going to turn her away.

I was trying to find any excuse not to go through with the robbery, but I saw the owner get on the horn and make a few calls, and a half hour later a younger-looking African girl pulled up to the door. I knew they would be in there for the rest of the night.

"Nah, I ain't scared, nigga. Just don't go in there getting all trigger-happy and shit like you did the last time. No one has to die."

Bunz turned and looked at me like he couldn't believe what I was saying, but I knew he got off on fear and sometimes didn't make the best decisions.

In a hostage situation your adrenaline is pumping, and the weed that we'd been smoking on all day made him think irrationally at the most inopportune times. That's why the last time we did a stick-up I found myself spreading peanut butter all over a dead woman's body while he yanked her teeth out of her mouth so that the rats and vermin would eat her and no one would be able to identify her body. Three days later they found the girl, and I tried like hell to keep a straight face as I watched the story breaking on the ten o'clock news, but it was killing me on the inside.

Lancaster Avenue was popping like it was three in the afternoon instead of the AM, so we waited until it died down some to make our move. Sporting all black with a Yankee's fitted pulled down over my eyes, we walked across the street like it wasn't nothing. The young girl and the client never saw us coming. We stood on the side of the door, out of their view, just to see who would walk up. I could see inside of the shop from my viewpoint, and although both the braider and the client were holding conversation, they both looked exhausted and ready to go home.

We were about to make our move when a bunch of loud, drunk-ass girls turned the corner where the newsstand was located after getting off the 40 bus. We didn't need any witnesses, so we waited for them to get up the block next to the barber shop before we did what we had to do.

"You ready, Street?" Bunz said to me under his breath, calling me by my last name.

I wanted to say that I wasn't ready, but I was already there, so I had to make it do what it was going to do. You could see the excitement of a possible kill in his eyes, but I was hoping he'd chill out tonight. Nightmares from so many dead bodies were already haunting my dreams, and I couldn't take it anymore.

"As ready as I'll ever be," I mumbled back, feeling the handle on the sawed-off shotgun I held in the small of my back.

From what we observed, there was a resident who lived on top of the braid shop that kept traffic coming in and out, so we just acted like we were waiting for him to come down and let us in as we stood in the cramped hallway outside of the shop, closing the gate behind us so that no one could just rush in.

Both the client and the stylist looked up at us, but quickly turned back to their conversation. I noticed that the woman who was getting her hair done was cute for a big girl, and under any other circumstances I probably would have tried to get at her. Tonight I was on a mission, but if I ever saw her again after this day it would be on.

The stylist must have said something to the girl because she had a scared look on her face, and the stylist stopped what she was doing and moved toward the door to lock it.

I was thinking, *Why in hell wasn't the door locked in the first damn place?* But she didn't even get a chance to touch it.

Bunz busted open the door and pulled his gun, causing the girl to stumble back to her chair.

My eyes were quick, and I saw the woman who was getting her hair braided dial some numbers on her phone and turn the volume down before placing her phone under the shelf, and I knew for sure she had called the cops.

Instead of alerting Bunz to the situation, I tried my best to speed it up because I knew the law was on its way, but if he knew that he would kill them. As he always said, "The dead can't testify in court."

"Give me all your fuckin' money," Bunz shouted at the two women, who were now shedding tears.

I felt like shit at that moment, but I needed this paper.

"There's no money here. They took it away earlier," the African girl said in a heavy accent.

I knew what she was saying was true. There was another African woman who could have easily been her mother in the shop with her earlier, and knowing the area that we were in, she more than likely took the money when she left.

"Let's just go, man. Ain't nothing poppin' in here," I said to Bunz, trying to quickly diffuse the situation. I can't do time. It just ain't in the cards.

"Man, fuck that," Bunz said with that wild look in his eyes he got every time a bad situation was about to turn worse.

A part of me just wanted to jet on his ass, but he was my boy, and besides all that, he had the car keys.

"Yo, I saw the other shorty leave earlier. She more than likely took the money with her."

"Yo, nigga, shut up. I know it's some money in this muthafucka, and that big bitch needs to empty her bag too. I know she got some rent money up in there."

I couldn't even look at her. Instead I looked out the window for any telltale signs that the jakes were heading our way, but everything was quiet. Looking back at Bunz, I could see him starting to get antsy, and his eyes had glazed over. Vince had told me about fucking with him, but my dumb ass didn't listen.

Just as I was turning my attention back to the situation at hand, I witnessed the brains of the young African girl fly from her head in slow motion and splatter in a bloody mess in the mirror. The client fainted on sight, but Bunz took it to her anyway. He put the silencer so close to her head, the spark bounced off her earrings, and at that very moment my stomach began to turn.

He rifled through her pocketbook and came up with about fifteen hundred dollars inside of a Bank of America deposit envelope. Either she just cashed her check or was going to deposit it. Too bad neither would ever go down.

Bunz looked around the shop, but found no cash. Cursing up a storm, he made his way back to the front of the shop, only to notice the open cell phone sitting under the counter. Going over to it, he picked it up to see 911 displayed across the call screen.

I just shook my head. It was one of those kind of situations where you ain't had no business doing what you were doing but you did it anyway and now look at you.

"Come on, nigga. Let's roll," he said after he turned the phone completely off and tucked it in his pocket.

When we got back to the car in front of the Lincoln Fried Chicken spot, he roofed the phone just in case it had a GPS hookup in it, and we got in the car and jetted.

Shanyce was gonna definitely be mad because the breakdown from that fifteen was only seven fifty apiece, and she needed our son Khalid's tuition money ASAP.

"Just drop me off on the corner, nigga," I said to Bunz as we approached my block. I had to face the music, but on the real, I wasn't ready.

About the Author

Anna J. is the author of three novels and six collaborations, including best selling work *My Woman His Wife*. She prides herself on being a "Philly Author," where she still resides, and is hard at work on her next novel, dropping in September of 2009. You can also find out more about Anna J. by visiting her website at www.askannaj.com.